I0682459

INTUITION

Jamie Weil

ISBN: 978-1-7334448-2-8
Library of Congress Control Number: 2019949596

Cover design: Jen Street

To my mom, who reads more books than anyone I know,
including this one more than once even though it was hard.
I love you. JJ

Acknowledgments

Each book is so unique. For me, I write a book because it pounds on my heart and won't go away. This particular journey was so personal because it was a story I had buried and refused to look at for so many years. Part of me didn't want to dance in the shadow of this thread because it was tied up with so many emotions, particularly sadness for the lives damaged and lost under such brutal savagery. I am grateful, though, to each person who supported me along the way, contributed to making it the best it could be, and touched the journey in some way.

Deep thanks to my mom who I think may have preferred not to have read this story multiple times as it was also a very traumatic time for her. Nevertheless, she bravely edited several versions, and championed my efforts along the way. My mom reads ten books a month (now on her Kindle!) which I find so inspiring. I hope one day I will be such a good reader as you, Mom.

So much gratitude to my editor and friend, Deb McCollett Harris, for her patience with me as I vacillated between traumatized teen and storyteller. Her gentle hand joined mine to make this story the best it could be without me losing sight of my job as a storyteller. Beyond that, she's just a beautiful soul and I'm so honored to have been able to publish my first novel, *First Break*, and this one with her as well. Talk about the frosting.

To Jen Street of Jen Street Designs who has now worked with me on branding four projects: Balsamic Moon Productions, my production company; *First Break*, my first YA novel: my docuseries *A Crazy Thought* about shifting the landscape of youth mental health; and now finally *Intuition*. Jen, you're a marvel at creating pictures from my rambling words. I'm certain I so inadequately throw them at you and yet you make them beautiful no matter what. Thank you for your intuition and talent in getting it right.

To that lead detective on the Darrell Rich case, Robbie Wharton, who encouraged me to write this book all those nights in the coffee shop while I was writing *First Break*, and who helped me fill in some blanks by pointing me to those who were there. Thank you, Robbie. Here you go. Sorry it took so long.

To all those who value and practice developing their own intuition, not for their own personal gains, but to lift the world's vibration, I see you. I know you're out there. I know you are building tribe, and I am 100% with you. We are creating a new world together that works for everyone and I'm excited. For all those that have helped me develop mine, deep gratitude.

This book is about more than just a serial killer and the savagery many faced at his hands. It's about friendships, relationships, and finding footing in those spaces, especially in youth. Early trauma is real and so many are reared in its bosom. We're told to put it behind us and move on. We now know, it demands that we face it lest it rear its ugly head in other seemingly unrelated diseases. Our greatest hope as we heal is to find whatever beauty we can glean to help others, to somehow make sense of the trauma. I feel so blessed to have friends that stand by my side, and who are there no matter what. To Netters, my best friend for the past 35 years, you are more valuable to me than all the world's riches. To Vin, Yols, Mel, Katherine, M, Sadie, Sissy, Janet, Janine, Kevin—I would crawl into a cave to save any of you. You have touched my heart in depths that I will remember through lifetimes.

Finally, to Team Weil, my five hearts that are the air that I breathe: Mike, Abe, Jordan, Kelly, and Kai. Thank you for surrounding me with such deep love. You melt my heart, and right now, I just want to go find an escape room and solve riddles with you. Left diamond!

"Our computers, our machines, our tools are not enough. We have to rely on our intuition, our true being."

~Joseph Campbell (p. xiv of *Power of Myth*)

Chapter 1

in·tu·i·tion
int(y)oo̅ˈiSH(ə)n/
noun
the ability to understand something immediately, without the need for
conscious reasoning.

Any other day, being last to leave the Jefferson Junior High parking
lot wouldn't have been a big deal. Today was different. Fourteen-year-
old Shay Burke bit the extra skin next to her thumbnail while she waited
with school gossip Kailee Watkins.

"Have you ever shot a gun?" Kailee asked.

"We're not really gun people," said Shay. She pulled her thumb away
from her teeth and shoved it in her shorts. Thirty days to break a habit
and she hadn't made it past two.

"You probably should become gun people," said Kailee, rubbing her
shoulder. "Dad dragged all three of us girls to the range last night." She
paused for Shay's reaction. "Everybody's losing it."

Murder did have a way of putting everybody on edge, Shay mused.
The air in Jefferson felt heavier after Julia Baird was found in a field of
poppies on the edge of town, propped up against a boulder, her skull
crushed in.

Shay nodded. "Did you know her? Julia, I mean."

"No. She was in high school."

Shay got it. The Untouchables usually didn't blend with the junior
high crowd. "Who do you think did it?"

"Don't know." Kailee shrugged. "My sister did. Know her, I mean."

Shay wasn't sure if Kailee was telling the truth or just fabricating a
personal connection again. "Wow. How'd she react?"

Kailee turned from Shay and looked toward the entrance to the
parking lot. "She was pretty upset."

"So weird." Shay couldn't really find the words to describe how she
was feeling about Julia's murder. Seeing killings on the news in other
places was one thing. It was horrible, but it didn't keep her up at night.
But nobody was ever murdered in Jefferson. Since she'd found out, she'd
noticed herself looking over her shoulder at every little sound. She'd
tossed and turned every night and could see circles starting to form
under her eyes.

"People are saying it's someone who lives here," Kailee interrupted Shay's thoughts. "Because of where they found her and everything." Kailee flung her backpack on her shoulder as her mom sped around the corner. "'Bout time. I'm late for dance."

Shay watched Mrs. Watkins pull into the lot in her semi-white, Ford pick-up. Dried mud splattered the side of the truck, remnants from a ranch run, no doubt. She screeched around the corner and yelled out the passenger window, "Hey, Shay, need a ride? I don't really want to leave you up here with everything that's been going on." Mrs. Watkins spoke almost too fast to understand and was always late for something.

"It's fine, thanks. Levi's mom should be here any—"

The truck peeled out of the parking lot taking the rest of Shay's sentence with it. As soon as Kailee was gone, Shay regretted not taking a ride. She pulled out her cell. Dead again. Her stepdad, Alex, had bought her this lame-ass phone off Craig's List. It couldn't hold a charge to save its life.

She'd give Carol a few more minutes to show up before she headed downtown to catch a ride home with Alex. That was the last thing she wanted to do. Just saying Alex's name pretty much made her want to vomit. Besides, practice had been exhausting and her legs felt like noodles. Most days, she regretted signing up for track. Running wasn't her thing. She'd done it mainly because Levi signed up, but he skipped half the time anyway. Coach Trimble had her race the two hundred because it wasn't too long and didn't require the speed of the fifty. That was her only event.

Right now, she just needed to sit. Shay flung her two-ton backpack down and flopped on the bench where she and Levi had made out many nights back in the days when it felt safer to troll after dark. Jefferson, population 1,592, didn't see much action. It was a pass-through kind of town, where travelers stopped for gas and peanuts. Most were traveling down Interstate 5, destined for some place more exciting. Julia Baird's murder had moved over sunny Jefferson like a huge dark cloud crammed with thunder and lightning. People were suddenly locking their windows and doors, getting concealed carry permits, and looking at each other out of the corners of their eyes. It was as if everybody was waiting for something, but they couldn't say what.

Shay shivered when she thought about the grisly way Julia had died. The *Jefferson Herald* told a version of the story. Shay had read the article twice. What it left out were the troubling details. She'd read those in the police report on Ronda's dad's desk while Ronda was in the shower and nobody else was home.

First, he'd bashed in Julia's head with a rock, but only after doing horrible things to her while she was still breathing. By those things, they knew he was male, although he hadn't left enough evidence behind to identify him specifically. Next, he placed her in a quasi-public area for viewing. Finally, he cut off half her nose, which authorities suspected he kept as a *trophy*. Redding P.D. had discovered her butt naked. At the hour they'd found her, she lay half in the sun and half in the shade, hands crossed in her lap as if she were sitting in the front church pew. Shay shuddered, then shifted her thoughts to Levi.

They'd been together since sixth grade, which by middle school standards was like two decades. Many of their friends had broken up and gotten back together more than five times, while their relationship grew stronger. Shay believed nobody could ever love her like Levi, partly because he told her that, and partly because she'd never felt more connected to anyone. Being connected to people had proven painful for Shay, like when her dad moved out and let Alex move in and ruin her life. She'd loved her dad and missed him terribly. Or like when the neighbor's oversized, mean-tempered dog had drowned her dog, leaving her to soak in her tears for weeks after. She'd decided then not to get close to anyone ever again.

But when she met Levi at the carnival during Rodeo Weekend, she couldn't resist his charm. He'd grabbed her hand and held it, sending a bolt of electricity shooting through her body like she'd never felt. He threw a ping pong ball into a goldfish bowl and won a pink elephant which she'd slept with every night since. At the end of the carnival, he pushed her up against the side of the feed store and whispered, "Will you be my girlfriend?" Feelings flooded over her and she could barely get out the word "yes," but when she did, he kissed her long and hard. It was a real kiss, with tongue and everything. She'd been hooked ever since. She loved everything about him: the way he tasted, his long dark eyelashes, the way his hand held the back of her head as they kissed.

Recently, things had changed. Her best friend Ronda had heard from Bobby Slay who heard from Kailee that Levi had been up at the lake rubbing suntan oil all over Veronica Vance. When she asked Levi about it, he'd said she was being ridiculous. But Instagram doesn't lie, and she'd seen the shots. Levi explained them away. She really wanted to believe him.

That was tough, though, because he didn't look at her like he had before. She could feel him slipping away. Even thinking about it made her throat tighten. She wasn't sure if she felt sad or mad that he'd promised to love her forever and was backing out now. Either way, she knew something needed to be done before their relationship dropped into the bottomless bucket of middle school breakups.

After ten minutes passed, Shay started walking. She was mad at herself for holding out for Levi and not taking Kailee's mom up on the ride. She needed to get to Alex's office before he took off. It was only about a mile down First Street, and she could make it well before dark if she left now. She slung her bag over one shoulder and tried to position the weight evenly as the strap dug into her skin.

To her right, a herd of sheep munched on yellow wildflowers and green spring grasses. The teachers at Jefferson made the students turn their desks away from the windows in the spring because the sheep would hump and students would giggle while making rude gestures. Shay liked looking at the field where lambs trotted together and played. She wondered what they thought about, what it would be like to be a lamb, not to have to worry about boyfriends and a killer on the loose.

As she went by the pasture and up the overpass on First Street, the view shifted to Interstate 5 with its whirring hum. Cars rushed north to Oregon and south to Sacramento beneath her feet. Even walking the ramp made her think of Levi. They'd taken his two little brothers across to buy them candy at the *Sports & Snacks* down on Main. The youngest one pulled down his pants and peed on the cars below before they knew what was happening. They'd laughed. Shay remembered thinking what a good dad Levi would be. For the rest of the day, she pretended they were parents, and Levi's brothers were their kids. They were a happy family and loved their children in all the *right* ways.

Goosebumps up and down her arms shook Shay out of her reverie. The gooseflesh made no sense, as the temperature was well past a hundred degrees outside. That quickly changed as she reached the top of the ramp. Shay felt a car inching up behind her. A pale yellow Plymouth pulled into her peripheral vision. She knew that car. It belonged to Wayne Garrett. She'd heard he was out. She'd also heard he was setting kittens on fire in Mr. Palmer's field just two days after leaving Crystal Camp. Before camp, he'd been caught shooting at cars on the old highway. She thought of his extensive knife collection. She'd watched it grow over the years. He always wore a black-handled blade strapped to his belt. He'd whipped it out during the County Fair on many occasions.

Shay's heart slammed against her chest. *Shit! There it is again.* She couldn't breathe. The sky started to spin. She stopped. The guard rail helped her balance. She'd been having these attacks for about a month. The first one hit when she found out about Veronica up at the lake with Levi. Freak-outs, she called them.

After the spinning slowed, she looked up. The car inched closer. Her calves burned. Her lungs ached. Each time she tried to get more air, she felt a stabbing pain. Next, she felt the strongest pull she'd ever felt. A silent scream. *"Don't get in that car. No matter what."*

As the car inched closer, Shay could see Wayne steering with one hand and leaning toward the passenger window. Both windows were rolled down.

"Oh, hi," she said, out of breath from scaling the hill, forcing a smile.

"Hey, Shay. Long time no see," said Garrett. "Thanks for visiting me at Crystal Camp."

"Of course," said Shay, giggling nervously.

Wayne Garrett smiled the type of smile Alex used when he was trying to get Shay to do something she didn't really want to do. Wayne pulled up next to Shay at the top of the ramp and stopped.

"Want a ride?" Icy blues flashed against shiny whites.

"No, it's okay. I need the walk," Shay lied. "I'm just heading over the hill to my stepdad's office. He mentioned you were out. How long's it been?"

His smile vanished. "A few weeks. Fucking Crystal Creek." His smile resurfaced. "Get in. I'll give you a ride down to the office. I got to stop in to see your dad anyway. Thank him for representing me."

"*Stepdad.*" Shay turned and shot him a glare.

"Sorry. *Stepdad.*" He made quotation marks with his fingers in the air. "No, really. It's no problem. Get in." His voice was insistent.

"It's okay." Shay's voice got higher and her smile more awkward. "I'm going to stop at *Sports & Snacks* anyway and pick up some gum."

"Did you say gun?" He pointed a gun at Shay. "Like this?"

He pushed forward down the ramp. The Plymouth screeched to a halt. Garrett threw the passenger's side door open. The door blocked Shay's path. He ran around the car. Shay froze. She was trapped between the car door and his body. He shoved her hard against the door.

"I'm not playing, Shay. Get the fuck in."

Shay watched every muscle in his face tighten and a vein pop out of his forehead.

"I'm not *asking,* Shay. *Get in the fucking car!*" He slurred his words. Whiskey. Shay smelled whiskey.

Wayne's eyes flashed. It was much different than the look he'd given her a few minutes before, the one that came with the charming smile. She couldn't look away until a honk broke the spell. She followed it with her eyes and saw Levi's mom driving up the ramp.

Levi's mom stopped at the top of the hill and Levi rolled down the window. "Hey, Shay, get in," yelled Levi from the back seat.

Wayne shifted his glare from Shay to Levi's car. He grabbed Shay and pretended to hug her hard as he whispered right up against her ear, "I know where you live."

Shay shivered, wiped her ear clean from his hot whiskey breath, wriggled out of his grasp, and ran to Levi's car.

"Sorry we're late. Brian had a game that went into overtime," said Levi. He threw open the back door and Shay jumped in. She scooted next to Levi. He put his hand on her shaking thigh. Her chest felt like she had just sprinted ten miles.

Wayne walked back around the car, and yelled in their direction, "Just catching up. We haven't seen each other in a while." He waved, jumped in the car, and drove off.

"Why were you hugging that creeper? Wasn't that the dude who just got out of juvie?"

"Crystal Creek," Shay said, her voice still shaking. "He's my babysitter's son."

Mama Mae had babysat Shay since she was six years old. When Shay's parents got divorced and her mom married Alex, they'd go on adult-only fishing trips up the Klamath. Shay would stay at Mama Mae's about a mile down the road and carry on with her regular school routine. She didn't mind it there because there were kids to play with. At home, it was just Shay, and that got lonely.

Mama Mae's son, Wayne, was one of those kids. He was older than Shay by about nine years. He'd played with The Daycare Kids, as he'd named them, in the irrigation ditches when they were younger. He pulled them on blue tarps across flooded pastures, whipping them around and carving figure eights in the tall grasses. He wore fitted white tanks and tanned the first day the sun came out in April. Each day he got darker and darker. Shay loved the way the sweat made the shirt stick to his body and made his muscles pop in the sunlight. To Shay, anybody older was cool, but she noticed something different about Wayne. She didn't dare tell anybody she had a crush on him, especially red-haired Sidney. She had her own freckled-face crush, and she was the only one he would let in his room with the door closed.

Levi's mom looked at her in the rearview mirror. "Shay, you should be careful walking around right now." Carol had three boys and Shay was the daughter she'd always wanted. She had a hair shop on the side of the house and would perm Shay's hair while they talked about Levi.

"I know, Carol. I just didn't know how I was going to get home." Shay flashed a glare at Levi who shrugged his shoulders and grabbed her thigh higher up. Shay shoved his hand away.

"Levi, why didn't you tell me Shay needed to be picked up earlier?" asked Carol shifting her eyes to him. "We could have left the game."

Shay knew by her response Levi was lying. It wasn't about the overtime either. More likely, Veronica had been there, and he'd been flirting with her out behind the stands.

"It's okay, Carol. I appreciate the ride anyway." Shay scooted away from Levi and looked out the window. "Would you mind dropping me at the office so I can get a ride home with Alex?"

Levi reached over to turn Shay's face back in his direction and made a pouty lip. Shay flashed a glare then turned back to the window. She really didn't want to go to Alex's office, but she was also fed up with Levi's games.

"You sure, honey? We're having your favorite. You know you're always welcome for dinner." Carol looked back at Shay in the rearview mirror.

Shay hated to disappoint people, and she could tell Carol wanted her to come over. "Well ... I do love your spaghetti."

Levi grabbed Shay's hand and wove his fingers through hers. He snuggled up against her and whispered, "I love you, Button. I'm sorry we were late."

Shay looked at him and nodded, trying hard not to tear up even though she felt it coming. She didn't like this namby-pamby part of herself. It made her feel weak. *Do I have no self-respect?* It wasn't perfect, but Levi made her happier than she'd ever been. And when she was with him, she wasn't so desperately alone. That was something.

"Want to walk over to the cemetery after dinner?" he whispered in the same ear Wayne had earlier.

She laid her head on his shoulder in an offering of forgiveness and smiled. That was code for "let's go make out in the casket vaults."

Chapter 2

im·pulse
ˈimˌpəls/
a sudden strong and unreflective urge or desire to act

When they walked into Levi's house, Shay realized why she didn't want to dump Levi. She didn't want to lose the Levi Package: the kitchen that smelled like crockpot spaghetti sauce, the tight-knit family, a double-wide made to look like a real home. Levi Sr. had built a tall wooden fence around the outside to make a safe place for Levi's little brothers to play. Shay felt that safety at Levi's, a feeling she didn't have at her own house.

Levi pushed open his bedroom door. Shay followed him inside. The room was small with just the basics. A card table in the corner worked as a desk. A black rolling chair they'd picked up at a garage sale sat in front. One of the wheels squeaked, but other than that, it was the nicest piece in Levi's room. A queen bed was shoved up against the corner on the opposite wall and took up most of the room, barely clearing the door.

The room sat right off the living room, which meant Carol let them close the door. Shay wondered if she'd still let them close it if she knew what went on in there. They threw their back packs on the card table desk, which buckled under the pressure of the weight. Levi took his cell out of his front pocket and set it on the table, screen down. He turned and pushed Shay down on the bed, straddled her, and started to take off his shirt.

"Leave it on," said Shay.

He frowned and pulled his shirt back on. He leaned over Shay and laced his fingers in hers, pressing her hands into the navy comforter. With his face just inches from hers, he smiled. "Still mad at me, Button?"

She hated it when he tried to be playful when he knew she was upset. It crossed a boundary that made her stomach hurt. Shay pulled her hands away, scooted up from underneath him, and positioned herself on her side. She burrowed her elbow into his pillows with the oversized 49er cases and propped her head up with her hand. "I'm not a sex toy, Levi. You can't just totally blow me off and then expect me to be all ready to go."

Levi moved up next to her and mirrored her position. He did the puppy dog thing with his eyes that he used when he was in trouble, making the same pouty lip he'd made in the car. Shay knew the cycle.

First, he was affectionate. Next, the nicey-nice good listener. Then, if she didn't respond the way he wanted, he turned into the blow-up bully and would go off on her. He didn't hit her, but he'd usually call her a bitch and other names he knew she hated. His goal seemed to be to make her cry, and he frequently achieved that. Or he'd just shut down. Sometimes he'd say he was sorry, but mostly he wouldn't. Shay could tell he always felt badly, though, and the end of the cycle always meant he was extra nice, caring, and usually gave her a present or a promise. A sort of memento of his shit behavior. It was exactly the same way Alex treated her mom.

Levi reached behind Shay's head and grabbed her blonde ponytail, tickling her cheek with the ends of her hair. He traced her hairline along the side of her face. "Why'd you ask Mom to take you home?"

"You know why." Shay laid her head back on the pillow to pull her hair out of his reach. Normally, she loved him playing with her hair, but right now it was just annoying. She wished she could just tell him to stop, but saying it directly was hard for her.

"You know I love you." Levi leaned over closer to her face and Eskimo-kissed her.

For a moment Shay felt that feeling she used to get at Viking Skate Country. Carol would drop them off for the evening session. They'd skip the skate pick up counter, and head straight to a corner behind the pinball machine. There they'd sit and stare at each other, lips gently touching, warm tongues dancing together to the loud music and lights. Then, they'd pull back, and look some more into each other's eyes like they were the only ones left alive. "You're so beautiful," he'd say, and Shay would feel her stomach fill with a thousand butterflies. Her Butterfly Moments, she called them. She could almost feel one starting now on Levi's bed, but that same thing that kept her from getting in the car with Wayne Garrett told her she should fight it.

Screw it. "I know," said Shay. "Especially when you want to hook up."

Levi would not be discouraged by her side bar. "You make it sound so cheap. 'Hook up.' I mean, if we died tomorrow, and we never did it … you want to take that chance? There's a killer on the loose, you know." Levi rolled on top of Shay and cupped her face in his hands. "Come on, Button. Do you?"

Levi's cell vibrated on his desk. He popped up, sat on the side of the bed, flipped it over to read it, then laid it back screen down.

"Really?" Shay's stomach tightened.

"What?" He plopped down in the squeaky-wheel chair and folded his arms across his chest.

Shay sat up. "You know what." She wanted to punch him in the face.

"I'm not a mind reader, Shay." He loud-whispered and Shay knew they were heading into Fight Land.

"Fine. Who was it?" she asked, even though they both knew she knew.

"Nobody."

"As in Vero-nobody?"

"What? No." Levi squished his face all up like he just smelled fresh dog poop. "You're unbelievable. I don't know why you even think I like her. You're so insecure." He leaned back in his chair, clasped his fingers behind his head, and propped his legs up on the bed. Shay wasn't in the mood for this thread.

It happened anyway. After what felt like an hour of the "you know I love you best talk," Carol yelled from the other side of the paper-thin door, "Lee, I need your help tracking down Eddie. He's already disappeared and it's almost time for dinner."

Levi looked at Shay and rolled his eyes. Then his face lit up. "This is our chance to hit the cemetery before your mom comes. I'll show you who I like." He leaned over and kissed her as if the previous hour didn't exist. He yelled back through the door, "Got it, Mom. He's probably over at the school shooting hoops. We'll go play with him for a while." He winked at Shay and grabbed her hand.

"Okay, great. First, can you help me get the big pot down for pasta?" she called back.

Levi kissed Shay and whispered, "Be right back."

As soon as he left for the kitchen, Shay grabbed Levi's phone and flipped it over. She put in her birthday to unlock it: 0313. Shit. He'd changed it. She tried his birthday: 1123. It opened up and Shay's heart dropped as she read: *sooooooo much fun today. can't wait 2 c u again, sexy. LOL. <3 V. Sent from Veronica's phone.* A picture of Veronica's boob followed.

Shay's heart started to pound like it had on the ramp earlier. She needed to think fast. She grabbed the phone and texted back, "call again and u die." She set the phone down exactly where it was and headed outside. She needed air fast or she was going to suffocate.

Shay stepped out in the yard and sat down on the front step. The late May sun calmed her some. She wanted to scream at Levi, to run away. But she loved him, and she didn't want to lose him either. She knew love was hard. Every songwriter said so. Every poet wrote about it. Every Nicolas Spark's book proved it. But in the end, love was stronger than all the other nonsense that came with it. It had to be.

The door opened behind her. "Where'd you go?" Levi asked, not waiting for the answer. "I bought us an hour. Let's go to our spot and hit the courts on the way back." To their left, they could see Eddie in the distance trying to shoot the ball into the high hoop underhand. "He'll be fine."

Shay stood up. Levi grabbed her hand and they walked across First Street to the Whispering Heights Cemetery. The cemetery was about fifty feet from Levi's house. Creepy, yes, but it also made for a pretty park-like setting. Large oaks filled the grassy areas. Brightly colored plastic flowers sat in copper vases and dotted the green with pinks, yellows, and faded red poinsettias left over from Christmas visits. Most of the headstones were small and flat, but every so often a fancier one popped up to announce the new dearly beloved living there.

A gravel road divided the cemetery in half. Along the road, Junipers stood tall, guardians of the dead cloaked in dark green. They created shady grassy areas which helped keep it cool as spring temperatures shot up. To the far left of the property ran a wider gravel road. Cars drove down it to get to the small parking lot in back, or for a drive-by visit. They'd enter, go slowly down the road, look out the window while signing the cross, and drive out the other side.

Behind the main house was where Carl, the groundskeeper, kept things. Nobody knew exactly what was in that house. Shay and Levi would see him walk out with a shovel in one hand and wave with the other. He always smiled and seemed proud they were visiting his graveyard. Carl rarely stuck around past four. That's when his old blue Ford sped down the gravel road and headed east on First.

In the far back of the cemetery was a wooden fence, weathered but still standing. Storms had knocked out several planks over the years. Through those openings, passersby could see the casket vaults. These large cement structures lay side by side like boats ready to transport the dead down the River Styx to the Underworld. The tops were open, and when Shay and Levi crawled inside, nobody could see them. Shay loved that secret place, away from the Veronicas of the world.

"Here," said Levi. He pushed down the bottom wire with one foot and pulled up the top so Shay could crawl through.

Shay crouched down as her legs screamed from the bear crawls. "I'm so done with track."

"Trimble go hard?" Levi asked, pleased with himself for skipping practice.

"Um, yeah." Shay stood up on the other side and held the fence for Levi. "Later I'm going to have to rub them out or they're going to cramp."

"That's what she said."

Shay rolled her eyes. They had about an hour left of pink daylight. In that hour they needed to have vault time, get Eddie, and get back before Carol got pissed. Shay's mom usually picked her up just after dark.

Levi motioned to the vaults. "Your fave."

Shay liked one in the back under the old oak tree. A branch from the tree hung about two feet from the vault and created shade. She walked toward it. Levi followed.

"You get in first," she said. "Make sure it's not too hot."

"You're too hot."

Shay shook her head. "Just … get in, you freak."

"That's what she said."

"One more time, Levi. I dare you. That's not even a thing." Shay couldn't help but grin as she said it. His dorky and dated playfulness was shifting her mood. "Say it one more time."

Levi smiled and took his phone from his back pocket. He handed it to Shay. He was already on his second phone and Carol told him that if he broke this one, that was it.

"Don't let me forget this. Mom will kill me." Shay grabbed the phone. Levi flipped off his thongs and jumped in.

Shay handed back his phone, put her shoes next to his, and flung her leg over the warm vault. She liked the feel of the warm cement on her thigh. It was so hard and solid. It knew exactly what it stood for, what its job was. It was brave and bold, nothing flimsy about it. Yet it embraced them warmly, gave them a place to love each other. She felt nurtured in the small space, cuddled up against Levi. Shay wished she could be more like the vault, badass and loving all wrapped into one. She didn't understand why she randomly felt like such a scaredy cat and why her body had been freaking the hell out at the worst times like on the ramp. She knew the vault never did that. It just sat there, strong and unchanging, waiting to fulfill its destiny when the time was right.

Levi lay down and Shay scooted on top of him. Their lips touched, then their tongues. Shay felt Levi's hands grab her lower back and pull her to him. Levi lifted up his shirt then Shay's. The feel of Levi's skin on hers made her shiver. As they pressed together, Levi moaned. He reached his hand up under the seam of her sports bra and pushed it up, finding as many spaces for their flesh to touch as possible without stripping down. Shay lost track of where she ended and where Levi started. Everything else faded and all she could focus on was this very moment she was in, Levi's lips and his body melting into hers.

Levi's hands moved down Shay's sides to her waist. He traced his thumbs slowly along the top edge of her board shorts and hooked them on each side of her hips, then pulled her into him again. He was as hard as the vault. He rotated his hips against hers and whispered in her ear, "I love you, Button. So much."

Shay thought maybe she'd been too tough on Levi. Maybe the whole Veronica thing *was* just her imagination. Kailee was a pot-stirrer anyway.

Maybe he really wasn't screwing around with Veronica at the lake. Maybe she just needed to give more so he'd never leave. She admitted she'd been holding back so she wouldn't get hurt, but maybe this was the time to take that next step.

"I think I'm ready," she whispered to Levi. Her heart beat faster.

Levi's breath was hot on her ear. "Here? In the vault? Seriously?"

"Seriously. I do love you."

Shay felt a surge of energy run through Levi as he unbuttoned his shorts and pulled down his zipper. She hoped she was making the right decision.

Shay grabbed Levi's hand. "Wait. Listen."

They held still and stared into each other's eyes. "Do you hear it?" Shay asked.

"No."

"Tires on the gravel. Somebody's here."

"Probably just Carl." Levi fumbled with his shorts. "Or a drive-by."

"It's too late for Carl." Shay held up her hand. "Stop. Wait."

"First you say yes, now …."

A car door slammed just on the other side of the weathered fence. Shay's eyes widened, and she put her finger up to her mouth. Levi nodded. She heard hard rock music and footsteps against the gravel. The footsteps were slow. Shay heard another sound against the gravel, like something being dragged. Then whimpers.

"Please, please don't," the voice begged.

"Shut the fuck up or I'll give you something to cry about." A voice Shay recognized.

"That's Wayne," she whispered in Levi's ear.

Levi's eyes opened wide and Shay could see fear there like she'd never seen it. A loud thump was followed by more whimpers.

Shay's heart pounded against Levi's. "I've got to look," she said.

Levi grabbed her tank and held her close as he mouthed, "Be careful!"

Working in the small space, Shay wiggled her way into a crouching position. The fence hid the vaults from the view of the car, but if the fence fell down at this very moment, they would have been laying only twenty feet from the whimperer. She thought she might be able to see from the top of the vault through one of the missing slats on the fence without being spotted. She knew it was Wayne, but she needed to know who he was with.

As she peeked over the top of vault, she could see through a slat where a board had split in half. That was enough to see the pale yellow Plymouth. The trunk was open, the windows rolled down, and the driver's side door was open. She couldn't see any people. She ducked back down.

"Shit. That's Wayne's car."

"Who?"

"Wayne. The dude that tried to pick me up today."

A scream, and a loud thump. Then silence.

Shay jumped back up and tried to look through her peephole from another angle. She saw his long, brown curly hair. His muscular arms were tan and bare. He wore a tight white tank and a pair of cut-off jeans with a black-handled knife in his belt. Shay could see Wayne bent over a somebody, doing something. She focused her eyes on the body. Lifeless girl legs splayed across the gravel. She could tell by the blue and yellow board shorts and purple Roxy flip flops. Wayne's body blocked the middle section, but on the other side of him she could see long black hair strewn across the gravel. She thought she was going to be sick.

She crouched back down and whispered to Levi, "He's not looking. See if you can tell who it is. I can only see part of her."

Levi scooted into a crouched position and peeked over the vault. Just as quickly, he collapsed back into the vault. He held his face in his hands.

"It's Veronica. That's what she was wearing today." He looked like Shay felt.

They both sat back up and saw Wayne get to his feet. His hands were covered in red and he wiped them on the sides of his white tank. He walked to the Plymouth and grabbed a roll of wrapping tape and a black bag. Shay's knees hurt from kneeling on the concrete, but she was frozen in place.

Wayne leaned over the body and started wrapping as if to keep the parts from flailing all over. Shay hoped this was the last step. It was too late to help Veronica. They'd have to wait. When Wayne drove off, they'd run across the junior high football field to Ronda's house. Her dad was the chief of police. They'd tell him right away who'd been terrorizing Jefferson.

The wrapping sound stopped, and the night was still for maybe ten seconds. She'd never forget what happened next. The loudest ring tone in the history of all ring tones started making a police siren noise, Levi's idea of a joke for his mom's custom tone.

Shay dropped down. "Shit. Turn it off!" she whisper-yelled, scrunching her face at him. It was too late. They'd been made.

"We need to get the fuck out of here," Levi fumbled his phone and dropped it.

The siren rang out again. Shay jumped up. Her eyes locked with two wild, icy blue eyes through the peephole. Wayne's eyes looked intense and hollow, like he was in a trance. Levi finally got his phone to stop and jumped up next to her.

Wayne kicked the fence hard. By some miracle, it didn't come

14

crashing down in one piece.

"Get over here, Shay. This is *your* fault. This should have been you," yelled Wayne in a fiery voice. "You even think about turning me in, I'll kill your mom and everybody you love slowly and tell them it was your fault."

"Run!" Shay swung her leg over the cement side and tore off toward the creek. She could hear Levi running behind her. The moon was huge and low in the sky, an eerie yellow color. Large river rocks made an obstacle course. Her ankles rolled as she tried to find footing in between stones. She could smell the creek ahead. She knew a place to hide.

Up ahead was a large, hollowed out log. Shay remembered looking there to collect insects for her science project. They would both fit— barely. Part of a Cottonwood tree, split by a January lightning storm, draped over the log making a perfect branch curtain.

"Over here," Shay yelled.

They squatted down and looked inside. A king snake slithered out. Shay shivered. She hated snakes. She hated killers even more. She backed in the log on her belly. Levi scooted in next to her. Shay could feel the bark scratching her bare skin.

"Ouch!" She put her own hand over her mouth.

"What's wrong?" Levi whispered.

"Fucking ants! Can you feel them?"

"Not yet." The log was dark inside, but the light shining in helped Levi see a huge spider hanging down right in front of him. "Forget the ants. Spider!" Levi crouched lower.

They hid in the log for what felt like hours. Shay's hearing felt sharper than ever. She listened to the flow of the creek, to Levi's breathing, to geese flying overhead. Then, new sounds: stones knocking together, and leaves crunching. He was close.

"I know you're out here with your little boyfriend, Shay. I know where he lives, too. I know his whole family. I'm not afraid to do to them what you saw me doing back there with your friend." Footsteps moved closer. "Come on out. I'm not going to hurt you. I just want to talk."

It was still a hundred degrees outside, but shivers shot through Shay's body. This wasn't just about her and Levi. This was way bigger. Other lives hung in the balance. Shay wondered if they were going to die in the log. Would he drag them out and prop them up, side by side, in the same poppy field where Julia Baird was found? Shay buried her face in her hands and tried not to breathe. She felt Levi's arm reach around her and stroke her hair.

"Come out, come out wherever you are." Wayne's voice sounded very close. "Remember when we used to play hide and seek in the barn? You always hid in the hay. I'd say, 'Hayyyyy, Shayyyyyy' and you'd giggle. I'd always find you. Remember, Shay?"

She did remember. Wayne could always find her. He would climb up in the loft, yell *"timberrrrr"* and fall two feet from where she hid, then grab her and tickle her until she couldn't breathe. Outside the log, the leaves of the Cottonwood tree rustled. He was shaking the branch. She hoped he couldn't hear her heart slamming against her ribs.

"Fine, Shay. I can't play all day. Just remember, I know where you live. If you say anything, you *will* be sorry. And that goes for you, too, sorry-chicken-ass-excuse for a boyfriend ... *and* your little brothers, too." He made a throat chortling noise like the witch from the east on *Wizard of Oz*. He and Shay watched that every Friday night when they were younger.

Shit. Shay's thoughts turned to Eddie. He was still out. They had to get to him before Wayne threw him in the trunk with Veronica. The crunch of leaves nearby made them tense up again. Shay saw sweat dripping down Levi's terrified face.

"Is he back?" Shay whispered.

Levi froze. Then a voice called out.

"Son, if you don't get your ass home right now, you're not going to be able to sit down!"

"Is that your dad?" Shay whispered.

Levi yelled, "Dad! Over here."

Footsteps tromped closer until two huge cankled feet stood in front of the open log. Senior stood nearly seven feet tall and tipped a solid three hundred on the scale. He moved like one of those Japanese Suma wrestlers Shay had seen in a special on the Discovery Channel. He bent over and looked in, his belly dropping down before his face.

"How'd you find us?" asked Levi, scrambling and leaving Shay in the log.

"The Garrett kid was nice enough to point me in the right direction. He told me to tell Shay he'd be over to visit soon. Said they go way back."

Shay shivered. Levi looked down at her with worried eyes. She looked up at the Levis and forced a smile. "Yeah. Thanks."

"Do you mind telling me what the hell you're both doing in there?" Senior asked, a vein popping out on his red forehead.

Levi paused before speaking. Shay wriggled out of the log and brushed off the ants. She could see Levi trying to figure out which parts to say and which to stay quiet about.

"We had this thing in science where we're supposed to collect a special kind of insect that only lives in these logs, but we weren't finding any, so we thought we'd wait until night and have better luck."

"Yeah, night bugs," Levi added.

Senior squinted and tilted his head at his son. Shay thought she saw

16

him bury a chuckle. "Yeah, right. I was young, too, you know. Let's keep this between us, you little love birds." He winked and dropped a meaty hand down to Shay. "It's past dark, and your mom is half out of her mind. Between you and that brother of yours … and Shay's dad waiting at the house."

Red welts lined Shay's calves where the ants had gone wild. After the first bites, she hadn't felt anything, but now numbness gave way to throbbing stings. They scanned the creek bed for signs of Wayne. Out here the only dependable light was the moon. In the last minutes after sunset, shadows cast across the river rocks from trees and bushes that lived near the creek. He could be anywhere.

Senior lumbered across the river rocks up toward the vaults. Without warning, Levi made a sharp right and started going back through the bus yard. Shay looked at him and he waved her to follow.

Senior looked back. "This way," he yelled. "What the hell are you doing? Quit dicking around."

"Can't we walk through the bus lot, Dad? It's quicker." The last thing Shay and Levi wanted to do was walk past the place where they'd seen Veronica.

"Oh, sure, Junior, let's take the scenic route." Senior plowed ahead. "What the hell's wrong with you?"

Levi looked at Shay and shook his head. There was no reasoning with Senior when he was irritated. Shay held her breath as they followed behind him, past the death boxes toward the barbed wire fence.

"After you." Senior pushed the bottom barbed wire down with his foot and pulled the top to make a crawl space. Shay and Levi climbed through. In a Houdini-like move, Senior held the fence in place and crawled through at the same time.

The full moon was close to the horizon now. It cast enough light so that Shay could see the Plymouth was gone. She could also see the marks in the gravel from the tires and the trail where Wayne had dragged Veronica's limp body. They moved silently down the center trail, past the Junipers, across the street, and into Levi's driveway.

Alex stood there with his ridiculous I'm-a-great-stepdad grin, always ready to show off in front of other people. Town politician and all. "Where you been, Shay-Shay?"

"Sorry, Alex. Won't happen again."

"That's my girl," he said, smiling at Junior and Senior and patting Shay's lower back. He opened the car door for her. "Hope you weren't doing something I wouldn't do." He let out a phony laugh and elbowed Senior, who joined in.

Shay looked at Levi who mouthed *I need to talk to you!*

"Oh, wait. I need my backpack," said Shay.

"It's already in the trunk," said Alex.

"Oh. Great." Shay slid in and stared forward, her stomach turning at the idea of a car ride with Alex.

He walked around and got in. Shay looked up and waved good bye to Levi. They backed out, and Alex reached over and put his hand on her bare thigh.

"Where's Mom?"

"Mom's going out tonight. It's just you and me, Shay-Shay."

Chapter 3

dys·func·tion·al
ˌdisˈfəNG(k)SH(ə)nl/
Adjective
1. not operating normally or properly.
2. Failure to grasp the consequences of a poorly thought
out decision.

The next morning, Shay was exhausted. She'd reviewed the overpass scene the entire night in her mind. She wondered why she hadn't gotten in that car. She felt horrible that Veronica had. She wondered when he'd picked her up. Was it just after he left the ramp? Had she made him so angry he had no other choice but to play out some sadistic obsession he couldn't control? She wondered what happened at Crystal Creek to change him into this monster.

"What's wrong, Shay-Shay?" asked Shay's mom as she pulled the SUV onto First.

That question was a trap and Shay knew it. Shay knew her mom didn't want an honest answer like "*Well, for one, you left me with my creepy stepdad who I didn't want in the first place and who I wish would fall off a tall building and splatter on the ground below,*" or, two, "*Well, I thought all night about Wayne—you remember Wayne, right?—and how he killed Veronica and probably Julia Baird and probably wanted to kill me and and may have all of us on his hit list?* She wasn't about to fall into the trap.

"Nothing, Mom. Just tired."

"Couldn't sleep?"

"Nope."

Shay leaned up to turn on the radio.

"Not too loud, Shay. I've got a headache."

Shay turned the radio off, lowered her seat back, and closed her eyes. After a few moments, she found herself listening to a talk radio host interviewing a serial killer. What were the odds?

Host: So when did you get your first urge to kill somebody?

Killer: Actually, I wanted to kill myself.

Host: Yourself?

Killer: My dad and I used to fight, and he would beat the shit out of me. The Daycare Kids hung on the fence and cheered.

Host: Wow. That's heavy.

Killer: That's when the anger started getting to be too much.

Host (part therapist/part interviewer): What else were you angry about?

Killer: When my mom and dad said they were getting a divorce.

Host: What did you do?

Killer: I shot myself in the chest.

Host: You told people it was an accident. Why?

Killer: Because I looked weak. I hate looking weak. That costs me every time.

Host: Like in Crystal Creek

Killer: This interview is over.

Shay's mom pulled into the parking lot. She shook Shay's shoulder. "You awake? See you tonight, sweetheart. Don't fall asleep in class."

A disoriented Shay jumped out. She didn't look back. She knew her mom was stressed, but so was she. She had to find Levi. They had to figure out what the hell they were going to do about catching Wayne. Shay hoped they could do that before he hurt anybody else. When she'd seen his eyes through the slat in the weathered fence, she could tell he'd lost all hope. He was desperate with a side of bat-shit. Not a good combo.

Her mind played back the text she'd sent from Levi's phone. *call again and u die. s.* Talking to anybody but Levi wasn't an option. They'd know the "s" meant Shay. Her feelings about Veronica were no secret. She'd definitely be a prime suspect. But if she told what she saw, she'd be putting herself and everybody else in danger.

There was only one solution. She and Levi would devise a plan to catch Garrett in the act. They'd snap shots on their phone. Catch some video of him kidnapping his victim. They'd upload it and the whole town would go vigilante on Garrett before anybody else got hurt. It'd be way more efficient than the understaffed Sheriff's Office. Besides, she'd seen it happen before. Buzz, the barber down on Main, headed up a whole gang of good old boys that met after dark down at the shop. They schemed about how to keep the town's Norman Rockwell vibe humming strong. They'd been known to fill in the gaps left wide open by budget cuts at the Sheriff's Office.

Shay went to the locker room to dress down for first period PE. When she walked in, Ronda was already there.

"Aloha, mi Ohana!" Ronda ran up to her and gave her a Big Island hug like she hadn't seen her for a year.

"Whoa. Hey." Shay steadied herself in the same way she did when Baron, the next-door neighbor's oversized German Shepherd, pounced on her. An obedience school dropout, he ran toward her with great enthusiasm when she came home. He'd then plant two front paws on her shoulders just so he could reach her face and give her sloppy kisses.

"You mean alohhhaaa," said Ronda.

Ronda had gone to Hawaii two years ago and she hadn't stopped alluding to it since. Her dad was the police chief and her mom worked as a heart surgeon at St. Mary's Medical. This meant, by Jefferson standards, she was a rich kid.

"Sorry. Aloha," said Shay, just to make it stop. "Where's my lei?"

Ronda laughed. "No lei today, but something better. Hurry up and we can be running partners."

Shay dressed in a hurry as Ronda waited impatiently, tapping her foot. She'd hoped to run with Levi so they could figure out their next move on Wayne, but she could tell that wasn't going to happen. Ronda was all amped about something and she wouldn't be able to shake her until she found out what.

"You're so freakin' slow, Shay."

"You got here earlier. Go ahead. I'll catch up."

"And leave my Ohana. No way, José."

"I'm not José," Shay mumbled. "She tied her shoes methodically, making every effort not to let Ronda make her antsy. Her laces were too long, and it slowed down the whole process. Ronda crossed her arms across her chest.

"What's up with Levi?"

"Oh, you know."

"Are you still together?"

"Why would you ask me that?"

"Just killing time." Ronda faked a yawn.

"I'm done." Shay jumped up and they headed out through the red door toward the field. "You really need to learn to chill."

Up ahead, Coach Trimble was rounding up the boys. Shay caught Levi's eye and cast her head toward the locker room door. He nodded and smiled. They'd meet there after track. Shay liked that Levi could tap in psychically every now and then. She tapped into Levi all the time. She didn't know how to turn that off, but she wished she did because it was super painful when he was cheating.

"Hey, over here," Kailee yelled from her place in the swarm of eighth grade girls clad in green. "Have you guys seen Veronica?" She studied the expression on Shay's face.

Shay looked at Ronda, who shook her head then looked back at Kailee. "Why?"

"She's not texting back and that's really weird. She's a texting maniac."

Ronda squared off with Kailee. "Who really cares anyway?"

It was no secret that Ronda disliked Veronica even more than Shay did. They'd had a fall out in sixth grade over Kyle Jenner. Ronda like-

liked Kyle and never forgave Veronica for stealing him away. Veronica bribed him with extra lunch dessert to get his attention. Ronda found out too late or would have found her own bribe, but the damage had already been done. Being Veronica-haters bonded Ronda and Shay. It was the main foundation of their new friendship.

In the town of Jefferson, there were only two schools, one elementary known as Jefferson East and one middle school officially titled Jefferson West. Everybody just called the middle school *Jefferson* as if by the time you'd reached middle school, you'd earned one-name status. Most of the students at Jefferson had history. They had gone to school together since they were four.

Friendships were reinvented when something went south. Every once in a while, a newcomer would come to town and try to break down the iron wall of familiarity. Veronica was one of those imports. She'd moved to Jefferson from New York at the beginning of sixth grade and fumbled between groups. Nobody would let her in. Shay felt sorry for her and asked her over one weekend. She liked the idea that Veronica was from somewhere else. That made her interesting. They started to hang out and share secrets. Because of Shay's endorsement, Veronica was able to gather friends—all of them Shay's—and actually have someone to eat with at lunch time.

When Shay discovered Veronica had been cheating with Levi, she was devastated. She'd never had a friend betray her like that after she'd had her back in such a big way. That's why she'd sent that text. It wasn't like her, but she'd lost it. She didn't mean it, of course. What had happened to Veronica—nobody should have had to endure that.

"Earth to Shay," said Kailee.

"Oh, what?" Shay blinked and zeroed in on Kailee's extraordinarily large teeth.

"Do you know anything about Veronica?" Kailee tilted her head and squinted her eyes like an interrogating detective.

"Why would I?" said Shay, pretending to look at something across the field.

Kailee shifted her weight to one side, put her hand on her hip, and started twirling the front of her hair with one finger in her I-know-something-you-don't-know pose. "Well ... because ... she mentioned you were mad at her."

"What? When?" asked Shay. "I mean, what are you talking about, Kailee?"

Ronda stood still, arms folded across her chest, and stared at each of them as if she were watching a ping pong tournament.

"She said you sent her a text from Levi's phone last night ... at least, she thought it was you."

Shay felt her heart beat fast and her face get hot. From across the field, a whistle blew.

"Ladies! Today!" Ms. Fenchler yelled across the field. "We're all waiting for you to grace us with your presence."

Shay and Ronda turned to run toward the lines. "What the hell was that about?" Ronda asked as they gained distance from Kailee who was taking her time walking across the field.

"I'll explain when we start."

Fenchler's stare shot across the class and hit Shay smack in the face. Shay looked down and tried to do the best warm-up she'd ever done, but she knew The Finch would ride her all period. Fenchler had earned her nickname due to her bird-like walk, her extremely big yellow bird-nest hair, and her beady bird eyes that flickered all over and saw everything. No teen unturned. The clinching finch detail was the manner in which she ate her protein bars. She'd pull them out of her shorts pocket half way during PE and peck at little bites, then dart her eyes around as she chewed. Pieces would fly out of her mouth like hulls off thistle seeds.

"And thanks to our three socialites, we'll be running an extra mile today," The Finch announced at the end of warm-ups. "You can thank Watkins, Burke, and Davis for that."

A loud groan accompanied eighty pairs of eyes casting daggers into Shay, Ronda, and Kailee. The Finch smiled.

"Get it done, ladies." The Finch blew her whistle and the sea of green moved to the red rubberized track. Shay and Ronda took off before Kailee could tail them. They knew they had to get a good half-track head start to get some privacy.

After they were well out of Kailee-range, Ronda started. "You sent Veronica a hate-text?" she asked between breaths.

If Ronda was anything, she was loyal, but Shay and Levi had sworn to each other they wouldn't tell. She chose her words carefully. "I reacted. She sent Levi a message and I saw it."

"What did it say?"

"I can't really talk about it right now." Shay breathed hard for effect.

"Can't or don't want to? Come on, Shay." Ronda reached over and hit Shay's arm. "I'd tell you."

Shay hated how Ronda bossed her around all the time. "Fine. What do you want to know?" Giving in was just easier than pissing her off.

"Is she cheating with Levi? Just like she's done with every other guy at Jefferson?" Ronda asked, and added, "I wish she would have stayed in New York."

Shay wanted to tell her. She needed to tell somebody. "I don't know. There was the lake thing. Then the text." Shay took a deep breath as they rounded their first lap. "I don't know who to believe anymore. Levi says

I'm making it up."

"I don't trust her, Shay. Never have."

Shay couldn't help thinking how unimportant that seemed in the face of what had happened. She just wished things had gone so differently. She wished she could trust somebody. Anybody. She wanted a redo.

"Can we talk about something else?"

"Okay, but one more thing. I don't trust Levi, either. You need to keep an eye on him."

Ronda and Levi had never liked each other. Levi came first before the friendship with Ronda really began. He resented the time Shay spent with Ronda. But when Shay tried to balance things out by spending time at his house, Ronda got jealous. Shay felt like an only child in the middle of a divorce. Each of them would talk smack about the other and she'd have to listen to all of it while defending one to the other. It sucked.

"You've never liked him. I'm sure it's fine. He loves me."

Ronda grabbed Shay's arm as it pumped back and forth, forcing Shay to look at her. "I love you, too, and you need to watch him."

"Okay, okay," said Shay.

"Besides, I'd really like to set you up with Ryan. Then when you get married we'll be—" she took a breath, "—sisters!"

Shay had passed the half-mile barrier and felt her breathing even out. "I don't even know your bro."

"You could, though."

"I'm still with Levi."

"Don't remind me."

They ran in silence for a lap. When she spoke, Ronda's voice sounded serious.

"Ryan hasn't dated anyone since ...."

"Since Julia?"

"Yeah."

"That's messed up."

"Right?"

"How long had they been dating before?"

"Not very long. Which made it all the weirder."

"Weird how?"

"Like they never had a chance to see what would happen." Ronda paused as her pace picked up to lose the girl tailing them on the turn. "I think he might have been in love."

"He's obviously not ready to date someone. That's only three weeks ago."

"I think it may help him. He spends all his time out in his damn shed."

"Shed?"

"It's out in the back behind the grapes."

"Doing what?"

"Staring at the walls? I have no idea. He has a big Keep Out sign on it. Mom says we need to let him have his space."

They had one lap to go. Shay hated running first thing in the morning. Her pits were soaked, and she'd have to take a shower or go through the day smelling like rotten shoes. Sticky hair lined the back of her neck and the sides of her face, but she wouldn't have time to wash it or she'd be late for English.

"Let's book it. I've got to—"

Shay stopped. She knew if she told Ronda she needed to talk to Levi, Ronda would sabotage it somehow. "Take a shower." Shay finished.

They sprinted the last lap, passing up much of the class. During minimum days like this, there was hardly enough time to change and change back, let alone run. Shay didn't mind, though. Anything to make the day go by faster.

On the way back to the locker room, Shay spotted Levi on the opposite side of the field.

"I'll meet you up there," she said to Ronda and jogged toward Levi before Ronda could say something rude.

As she got closer, Shay noticed Levi flirting with Emma Sanders. She felt her stomach knot as she watched him touch Emma's lower back. Not sure whether to charge and kick him in the back of the knees or just ignore him entirely and run toward the locker room, she decided she'd had enough. She walked directly toward him with purpose.

"Oh, hi, Shay. Emma and I were just—"

"I know what you and Emma were doing."

Emma giggled and turned away. "See you, Levi."

Shay watched her leave then turned back to Levi. "I'm so done."

"With me? Just like that?"

"Really? Every time I turn around you're flirting with someone else. Veronica's dead less than twenty-four hours and you have to find another cheating partner?" Shay noticed him flinch when she said Veronica's name.

"I thought we were going to catch this creep together," he said so softly that Shay almost felt sorry for him.

"You're the creep." Shay turned to walk away. "I'll do it myself."

Levi yelled after her, "You?"

Shay turned back and stared. "What's that supposed to mean?"

Levi fake-laughed. "I don't see it. Besides, I've decided I'm going to go to the cops."

Shay felt her heart start up. *Not now!* Just the feel of having one of her freak-outs made her eyes well up.

"See? What are you going to do, Shay?" Levi had this way of intentionally stinging her when she was in her most vulnerable place. "Drown him with your tears?"

The Finch walked up behind them.

"Problem here, Love Birds?" She looked at Shay's face, then back at Levi. "Trouble in paradise?"

"It's all good," Levi said in his flirty voice. "Your hair looks great today, Ms. Fenchler."

The Finch smirked. "Okay, Casanova. Just get to the locker room and shower so you're not late for next period." The Finch turned to leave as Shay glared at Levi.

Shay watched The Finch walk away then shifted her eyes back to Levi. "You disgust me."

Levi shrugged and walked away, leaving Shay to wish she'd walked away first.

***

Even at nine a.m. on a May morning, the sun beat down a sweltering ninety degrees on Jefferson Junior High. The end of eighth grade was supposed to mark a time spent with class trips, days on the green, and graduation parties, not break-ups, funerals, and school budget cuts.

Shay sat with her eyes glued to the silver crossing lines on the ceiling of Portable 3. Portable Row had come in when the school had more money, but last year, when five of Jefferson's senior teachers were given pink slips, it sat mostly abandoned with one exception: eighth grade English. She studied the pockmarks on each tile piece as Ms. Montag read *To Kill A Mockingbird*.

They'd been listening to the book for what seemed like forever and they'd finally gotten to the trial where Atticus was questioning Tom Robinson after Mayella Ewell swore Robinson had "taken advantage of her." Shay had several thoughts. First, she wished Alex could be more like Atticus. The way he let Scout climb up on his lap and read from the time she was young, and not in a pervy way which was how Alex did everything. Atticus seemed so kind and gentle, so smart and sophisticated.

Second, she was pretty sure they still read this book in her town just so they could repeat the N-word over and over. Jefferson had a sign posted on the road into town that read "No Room for Racism" with a bullet hole right through the middle. Granted it was no 1930s South, but perhaps a close cousin that still retained some of the region's DNA. White people made up the town, with a splattering of blacks that seemed to come and go in very small numbers. Calvin Collins was one of those boys. He sat two seats behind Shay in English. She wondered how he felt when Ms. Montag said the N-word and the class snickered under their breath. Did he feel like society was different now, nearly a hundred years later?

And, third, Shay wished she could be more like Jean Louise with her cool nickname. Scout was badass. Shay knew if Scout popped over from Maycomb to Jefferson—after time-traveling from the 1930s—she could help her stop Wayne Garrett for sure. She was pretty sure Scout didn't have freak-outs. *That* would be useful. Scout was only in first grade and she seemed fearless. Maybe living during the Great Depression made people stronger. The shy part of Shay, the part that kept her from feeling strong enough to stand up to the people when she should, was her least favorite part of herself. She really admired that strength she saw in Scout.

Ms. Montag read and Tom Robinson presented his defense. Shay liked the sound of Ms. Montag's voice. It calmed her. It felt warm and safe, like when her mom used to read her bedtime stories. And calm was a good thing, because in the passing period following second, all hell broke loose.

Chapter 4

so·cial me·di·a
\ ˈsō-shəl\ \ ˈmē-dē-ə\
noun
Your electronic Second Life.
Best described using examples:
Facebook-I like doughnuts
Twitter-I'm eating #doughnuts
Instagram-Here is a polaroid-esce photo of doughnuts
Foursquare-This is where I eat doughnuts
Youtube-Here I am eating doughnuts
Myspace-Meet the Up-and-coming band, 'doghnuts'
Linkedin-My skills include doughnut eating
Pinterest-Here is a recipe for doughnuts
And on and on and on, in constant reinvention

As soon as the bell rang, Shay pulled her phone from her pocket. She'd felt it vibrate when Ms. Montag was finishing up with Tom Robinson's testimony, but she didn't dare pull it out. That's how phones ended up in the office.

She looked down at her front screen. It was completely blown up. Kailee's text was first and caught her eye.

Did u hear about VV?

As she hurried out of the classroom, Ms. Montag called after her.

"Got a minute?" she asked.

Shay froze. She definitely didn't have a minute, but she knew that was the wrong answer. "Um, yeah."

"I was checking my notes and you have some books out. Are you aware?"

"Oh, yeah." She had totally forgotten. She had no idea where they were. "Sorry."

"No problem. You just need to get them into the office to graduate. Or pay for them. Just go in after school and take care of it."

"Sure. Thanks." Shay shoved her phone into her jeans pocket and heaved her backpack over her shoulder. She needed to find the books. She didn't have time to move through the portals and feeds.

The hallway was buzzing. Teens gathered in tight groups, huddled over their phones, hanging near their lockers. Something big was going down. Shay scanned the hall for Kailee or Ronda but didn't see either. She remembered she'd also had a text from Ronda and figured that might explain where she was.

Check out feed.

Shay switched to Facebook and frantically scrolled down through the feed.

KP: 8 hours ago. Anybody seen Veronica? With Sadie Sanders and Shea Pater. Four comments followed with a series of emojis:

Mariah: Sorry boo cakes:(

Jess: its bad

Brandon: whats going on

Scott: heard she kicked it

Winter: ?????????

Sarah: popo found ded n8kd

Riley: shit

Kailey: omg omg omg

The thread went on to say Veronica's body had been found covered in nothing but bite marks. She'd been thrown off the bridge at John's Creek near Shasta. She'd crawled halfway up the bank and eventually into the fetal position. Shay felt her body go cold. Even though she'd already known about Veronica, seeing it on the feed made it so permanent, so real.

Shay was confused. When she'd seen Veronica, she'd thought she was dead. That made not telling somebody that much worse. What if she could have prevented Veronica's brutal exit? The police were all over the place trying to figure out who did it. They said they were following multiple leads, code for they didn't have a clue. If Shay knew for sure they could catch Garrett she'd come clean in a heartbeat and tell them everything. She wanted to feel that confidence, but she didn't.

"Shay," Ronda yelled from down the hall.

She hurried toward Ronda as Ronda ran in her direction making sure none of the teachers saw her do it. Ronda hugged her and whispered, "Oh, my God. Did you see what happened?"

"Yes," Shay whispered back.

"I called my dad. The worst part is they have no idea who did it."

That was not what Shay wanted to hear. She pulled back and looked at Ronda. "Nothing?"

"Dad said Alex and he have to talk about some things tonight. Brainstorm, I guess. Come over after school and we'll talk about all this." Ronda grabbed Shay's shoulders tight. Her big blue eyes lined with too much eyeliner did not hide worry well.

"Sounds good."

"Just meet me outside math."

"Oh, wait. I just remembered I need to go to the office. I've got to pay off my books."

"I'd wait for you, but I have to be home to let the cable guy in. Mom texted me. Ryan wasn't answering per usual."

"No problem. I'll meet you at your house."

The rest of the day dragged. The tension was thick. Shay was so grateful it was minimum day. All her classes blended together, and she couldn't focus enough to catch anything the teachers were saying. Instead, she rehearsed what was going to happen after school. She would take care of her books, pick up her gown in the office which they were withholding because of lack of book payment, then run to Ronda's. When she got over to Ronda's, she'd tell her everything she knew about Wayne Garrett, and together they'd figure out how to stop him before he killed anybody else.

At twelve thirty, the halls of Jefferson Junior High were packed with students making a mad exodus for the long Memorial Day weekend. Bulletin boards lined the walls with "Congratulation" signs for the graduating class and reminders that the graduation dance was only available to those with a 3.0 or higher who had all their fees paid in full.

When Shay walked in the office, she quickly realized she wasn't the only one who'd forgotten about her library books. Kailee was five people back. Shay lined up behind her. Ms. Martin was arguing with a student at the desk. Kailee spotted Shay and her eyes lit up.

"Did you hear?" she whispered.

Shay thought maybe Kailee didn't realize everybody knew she was the school gossip and that was why she whispered. "I think everybody's heard."

"Can you imagine going like that? I heard he picked her up in town."

"Who told you that? Who picked her up?"

Kailee's eyes sparkled as she realized this was a new detail for Shay. "Bobby Vance's mom saw her get in the car with some guy."

"What guy?"

"She didn't know, but it didn't look forced or anything."

"Then maybe it wasn't the right guy," said Shay.

"Why?" Kailee paused on cue. She fished for more information she could vomit on the masses. "Do you know something else?"

"No. I don't know anything."

From behind the desk, Ms. Martin yelled, "Next." The student she'd been arguing with stomped off with an attitude and without a gown.

"Are you and Levi going to the graduation dance?"

"Um, we … yeah, probably." *Tread carefully, Shay.*

"Lucky."

"You're not going?"

Another "Next" moved them closer.

"Yeah, right. With who?"

Shay struggled to find the right words. "I think groups of people are just going together."

Kailee looked sad and Shay wanted to fix it. "You should come. It'll be fun."

"Next."

"Maybe you're right. Thanks, Shay."

The last thing Shay wanted to do was go to the stupid dance. All the year-end activities she'd been looking forward to since sixth grade seemed so empty now. She didn't have Levi, which was bad enough, but with what had happened to Julia and to Veronica—and almost to her—eighth grade dances and picnics seemed ridiculous. She wouldn't be able to enjoy herself until Wayne Garrett was behind bars.

Kailee finally made it through the line to the front desk. Shay checked her cell. Figured. Almost dead.

"Next."

Mrs. Martin stared up at her through black horn-rimmed glasses. She appeared close to a hundred, with tall white hair that never made it out of the '60s. Bright red lipstick highlighted her nicotine yellowed teeth. She had more wrinkles than Kona, Ronda's new Shar-Pei puppy. Her neck had a wattle hanging down that reminded Shay of the wild turkeys that roamed the pastures of Jefferson. Each day of the week she wore a different color of bright floral bell-bottoms. Today was hot pink. Shay wondered if anybody else on the planet still owned floral bell-bottoms.

"Ms. Burke. I see you have some books out?"

"Yeah. I can't find them."

"That'll be twenty-two dollars."

Shay cringed. She'd mowed the lawn for this money. She'd hoped to buy something good, not pay fines with it. What a racket. She could have bought the book for cheaper than that.

"Sure," she said, pulling a twenty and a five from her wallet then getting three dollars, a gown, and a "Next" for her investment.

The clock read 12:35. Ronda would be home by now. Shay hurried out of the office and pulled out her phone to text her.

Text to Ronda: On my—

Her screen went black. Shay threw her head back and looked up at the sky. Her backpack was stuffed, but she didn't want to carry the gown. She unzipped it and started reorganizing. If all the books pushed to one side, she could slip it down on the other without busting the zipper. The bottom seam was ripping, but if she could just make it through the next few weeks, she wouldn't need to get a new one. Mission accomplished.

Shay looked down at her watch, proud of herself for remembering to wear it. She'd get to Ronda's by one if she cut through the baseball field, followed the creek, and crossed the main road into the subdivision. As she moved quickly down the stairs, past the gym, and toward the baseball diamond, she thought about how the conversation with Ronda would go.

Shay: I want to tell you something.
Ronda: What?
Shay: I know who killed Veronica.
Ronda: How? You're just telling me this now?
Rewind. Delete.
Shay: I know who killed Veronica.
Ronda: How?
Shay: I saw it.
Ronda: What? When?

That wasn't good, either. Shay played through ten more scenarios in her mind as she walked. As she approached the main road, she spotted the Plymouth cresting the ramp. Her heart pounded. She jumped back behind a tree. She peeked out. He sped toward her. It was definitely him. This time, he'd kill her. She was trapped. She knew it. The thought of getting her skull crashed in after he'd—

She bolted across the main road. The screech of wheels behind her made her sprint. She shot into Ronda's neighborhood. Her feet slammed against the pavement. Her lungs burned as she gasped for air. She smelled the gas as he revved the engine. He could overtake her in his car. She darted left down the gravel path that lined the canal. He couldn't drive down there. She heard the car door slam behind her. Wayne screamed her name. Shit. She was on the wrong side of the canal. A bullet smashed against the wooden fence on her left. She threw off her backpack. Shay held her breath and heaved herself across the canal.

She missed the bank. The water froze her skin. It pushed all her air out. The black engulfed her. Long hair wrapped around her face like seaweed. Open hands clawed at the water. The current tumbled her in every direction. Eyes squinted to find the light. When they did, Shay flailed her arms and legs as fast as she could and broke the surface. She gasped for air.

A pipe jutted out from the bank just ahead. Shay readied her hand and heaved her right arm high above the current. Her fingers wrapped around the pipe. The hot steel seared her flesh. She cried out. Her wet fingers started to slip. She forced herself to grab on with the left hand. It was the only way out. She heaved herself onto the bank. Shay looked back, eyes stinging from the water. Her backpack was a good distance back. No time. She rushed toward Ronda's back fence. The gravel underneath her feet made her feet slip as she ran. Another shot fired. She heard the ting of the bullet on the chain length fence to her right.

Ronda's fence towered over her. With hands still stinging from the pipe, she grabbed the top. Her hands throbbed in pain. Her feet scrambled against the wood. She pulled herself up and over just as another shot exploded. She felt the vibration on the fence from the bullet. Her lungs were on fire. She flopped to the other side and crashed face down on the rocks.

Shay heard a snap. Her ankle throbbed. Her heart pounded her rib cage. The sky started to spin. Her legs went numb. She pushed herself up to all fours. Sharp rocks stabbed her knees. Shay crawled down dirt paths lined toward a little house in the back with a "KEEP OUT" sign.

"Help," she whispered.

Ronda's house was on the other side of the small vineyard. She could make it. As she passed the shed, she noticed the door was cracked. She crawled around and peeked in. Ronda's brother was sleeping on a cot in the corner, earbuds in his ears.

She felt wet on her cheek and turned to see Kona wagging his tale enthusiastically. The pup lathered her with kisses despite the fact she stunk like rotten fish.

Chapter 5

pup·py love
noun
\ˈpə-pē\ \ˈləv\
an intense romantic attachment, typically associated with
adolescents.

Shay woke up to two pairs of deep brown eyes staring down at her: Ryan's and Kona's. She was lying on the cot. Ryan was sitting next to her holding Kona on his lap.

Ryan was a sophomore at Jefferson High. Shay had only seen him at a distance around town. Her loss, clearly. He was beyond hot. He wore his loose auburn waves long. His hair swept to the side just above his hazel eyes which looked green against his tan skin. His jawline showed signs of true stubble, not the eighth-grade kind the boys at her school loved to talk about. He stood about half a foot taller than she. He looked strong without looking obsessed with the weight room. Cut in all the right places. Shay looked around the room and hoped her cheeks weren't as red as they felt.

"Hey," he said softly.

"Oh, hi," Shay said sounding younger than her fourteen years. She cleared her throat. "What happened?"

"Yeah. I was going to ask you that." Ryan smiled at Shay and when he did, she noticed he also had a slight dimple in each cheek.

"I love your," Shay paused.

"What?" He smiled even bigger, deepening his dimples. His gentle way of talking comforted her.

"Your shed." Shay wanted to hit herself in the forehead for her inability to flirt. Somehow shed seemed safer than dimples. "Quite a place."

The walls of Ryan's shed were rustic and empty with one exception: a wall behind his desk that looked like a scene out of "Law and Order." A huge white board with multiple colors of dry erase markers covered the wall. Colored magnets held up different pictures. Pictures of Julia and Veronica hung side by side.

Ryan's eyes followed Shay's to the board. When she looked at him, she noticed how sad they looked now. "Ronda said you went out."

"With Julia? Yeah."

"I'm really sorry. That must be so hard."

For a moment, Shay wondered if she'd said the wrong thing. The shed was filled with silence. Ryan studied his flip flops. Kona heard a goose honk overhead, gave one bark, and ran out the door.

"It's okay. You want to tell me how you wound up in my shed?" Ryan pointed to the sign and put on a fake serious face. "Did you not read the sign?"

"Yeah, about that," said Shay. "If I tell you someone was shooting at me, do I get a pass?"

Ryan's face shifted to serious for real this time. "What?"

"I was supposed to meet Ronda here. I was crossing the main road when I—" Shay didn't even know Ryan. If time was the barometer, she barely knew Ronda. Their dad was chief of police. She looked down at her ankle, which was the size of Jupiter, and decided she needed help. It made no sense, but she'd have to come clean.

"When what?" said Ryan impatiently.

"When I saw him coming over the ramp. He chased me down the back road along the canal and shot at me." Shay's voice started to shake from adrenaline.

"Who's *him*?" Do you know *him*?"

"Yes. Wayne Garrett." As soon as she said it, Shay felt both terror and relief. Terror because if Garrett found out, she knew he would keep his promise. Relief, because now she was not carrying the burden alone.

Ryan stood up and walked over to the white board. He wrote WAYNE GARRETT in red letters next to the question mark. "That totally fits. If it's him, we're safe here. He won't come around my dad."

Shay felt purpose mix with possibility. Ryan and she could work together to get Garrett behind bars. "There's more. He tried to pick me up yesterday. Later, Levi and I saw him in the cemetery with Veronica. She was dead."

"Wait, what?" Ryan looked confused. "Why were you even in the cemetery?"

Shay hesitated. "We … um … we make out in the casket vaults."

"Oh, that's just wrong," said Ryan. "So when did you see him?"

"We heard him first. We looked up and saw him wrapping Veronica in tape or something."

"Did you call the cops?"

"No."

"You *didn't* call the cops? What the hell?" Ryan held up his hands.

"He knows me, Ryan. His mom used to babysit me. I grew up with him. And he threatened to kill my family."

Ryan started to pace, then came back and stood over Shay at the edge of the cot. He reached over and pulled a leaf out of her damp hair. "I'm glad you got away."

"Me, too. But I feel horrible about Veronica."

"Me, too."

Shay thought for a minute. "No, but you don't get it. I just hated her because Levi cheated with her."

"No, I get that." Ryan nodded. "I get jealous, too."

"Except that I made mine public."

"What do you mean?"

Shay shook her head and bit her lip. "I sent her a text and told her I wanted her dead."

Ryan stared at Shay then up at the board, pausing to carefully choose his next words. "Then you'd be a suspect, right?"

Shay was fairly sure all dating options were now off the table. "You tell me. But, yeah, I think so."

Ryan sat eerily still and looked straight ahead at the wall. After a pause that felt like an hour and was probably a half minute, he turned toward Shay and broke the silence.

"We need to tell my dad, Shay."

"Ryan, no. Please not yet. I'm afraid they won't believe me, and they'll think I did it. Then I'll go away to juvie and Garrett will kill my family for sure."

Ryan nodded. "Not gonna lie. That could happen. I'd try to protect you, but—"

Shay jumped up and gave him her most assertive look. "I really think we could get this done quicker if we just try to catch him. I know how he thinks."

"You're probably right." Ryan passed her the leaf he'd pulled from her hair. "Yours?"

"I took a little swim in the canal. There's a lot more stuff floating around in there than you'd think."

Ryan nodded. "Just below the surface. Were you friends? You and Garrett?"

"No ... well, we were at one point. Then we weren't." It all seemed so stupid now. Shay was embarrassed to elaborate.

"And he still threatened to kill you and your family if you told?" Ryan's voice took on a detective quality.

"Yes. And he'll do it. He would have killed me today," said Shay. "I think he's unravelling."

"What makes you say that?"

"I've seen enough *Criminal Minds* to know when an unsub is escalating. He brutally attacked Veronica then threw her off a bridge. You know that, right?"

Ryan stared at the board. "Yeah. I overheard Dad talking on the phone. She was alive when she hit the water and crawled to the bank of the river. She was only wearing her panties when they found her."

"Up at John's Creek, right?"

Ryan nodded and wrote JOHN'S CREEK in green next to Veronica's name. Shay watched his tan muscles flex as he wrote. She wondered what it would feel like to kiss him. She felt ridiculous for having that thought in the center of this chaotic moment. She sat back down on the cot. He put the marker down and walked toward her.

"May I?" he asked and pointed to the point on the cot next to her.

"Why, yes." Shay smiled and felt her chest flutter. "You may."

Ryan sat down closer than Shay anticipated. He wore tan cargo shorts against a white tank. When he sat, his shorts hiked up past his knees and she became aware of his tanned, muscular legs. She could feel the heat from his calves which he stretched out next to hers. Shay had always felt intimidated by older boys, but she liked the way Ryan acted more mature.

Ryan tapped Shay's foot with his black Rainbow flip-flop, which made her smile. "What's going to happen with you and this Levi kid?"

"We broke up," Shay said quickly.

"As in *really broke up* or as in *you're getting back together on Monday* broke up?" Ryan said it casually like he wasn't invested either way. It was one of the things Shay liked about him. He talked to her with respect.

"I'm so done." Shay stared at her feet and shook her head. "He's not a good boyfriend."

"How so?"

"He lies."

"About what?" Ryan tapped Shay's foot again. His voice sounded concerned.

"Other girls mainly."

"That's cold," said Ryan.

"Yep. He's cheated on me one too many times. I feel stupid for still feeling so upset about breaking up."

"It takes a while for these things to work their way out," said Ryan quietly. "I would never cheat on you."

Shay smiled. She felt she should say something more about Julia, but she couldn't find the right words. She hadn't known anybody else who had died except for her grandpa and that happened when she was a week old. Saying the right thing was especially hard because she sensed Ryan loved Julia. Having her die so suddenly and so viciously would screw with anyone's mind.

"Is that happening for you?" she finally got out. "I mean, is it working its way out?" As soon as the words got out, she felt they were insufficient.

"It's hard." Ryan's voice cracked. "We were in that new place where everything works. That falling in love bliss, you know?"

Shay thought back to the early days with Levi. "I love that time. Everything just fits. Colors seem brighter."

"And then they turn black," said Ryan. "That's why I'm not going to rest until this asshole is strapped down on a table after his last meal."

It hadn't occurred to Shay that Garrett could get the death penalty. "Me, neither. I'm going to help you."

"Hey, I just thought of something. First step in Project Garrett."

Shay repositioned so she was facing him directly. "What?"

"Well, Dad's talking to your dad tonight, right?"

"Stepdad."

Ryan paused. "Sorry. Stepdad. You don't like him much?"

"No."

"Okay. I get that. When they're talking, we can record their conversation and get deets. We can use those to work out our plan."

"Perfect. What about Ronda?"

Ryan hesitated and ran his fingers through his hair. "Should we tell her?"

"Of course. She's my best friend. I'd feel like a creep excluding her."

"She's got a big mouth, though." Ryan opened his eyes wide and nodded his head, as if he was agreeing with his own insight. "That's my concern."

Shay studied the white board for a moment. Ronda could be bossy and had a hard time keeping a secret, but she was a loyal friend. Besides, they could use all the help they could get. They needed to get this maniac off the streets yesterday. "We should include her. She won't say anything. Besides, threes are magic, right?"

"Magic?"

"Yeah, like three little pigs, Goldilocks and the Three Bears, the Three Musketeers—"

"Three blind mice?" Ryan chimed in.

"Shit, I hope not." Shay let out a nervous laugh.

"It all comes back to the fairy tales, doesn't it?" said Ryan.

"Yep. I guess it does." Shay hadn't really thought about that before. Life didn't feel like a fairy tale the way it played out for her.

"Let's go and see if we can track that girl down," said Ryan.

Ryan shut the shed and headed through the garden into the house. Shay limped behind. They walked through the garden and around the kidney-shaped pool. Shay had forgotten how badly her ankle hurt and how wet she was until they started moving.

"Ouch!" She bent down and grabbed her ankle.

Ryan turned around. "Oh, crap. Sorry. Here. Let me help you." He rushed over, draped her arm across his shoulder, and pulled her into him. "You're soaked!"

"And now so are you," she said.

He opened the slider to the Reynolds' home. "Princess Ronda," he yelled, "come out of your castle. A little help."

Ronda walked around the corner wearing her fighting face. It vanished when she saw Shay. "Oh, my God, Shay, what happened?"

"Long story," said Shay, limping to Ronda as Ryan passed her off.

"Are you okay?"

"Better now."

Shay hobbled into the bathroom. She used the toilet as a chair while Ronda fumbled around for towels. Shay told her story. Every detail poured out unfiltered. She told Ronda about Wayne Garrett, about how he'd tried to grab her. She told Ronda about how Levi and she had broken up. She explained how she and Ryan were pretty sure Wayne Garrett was the killer and how they needed to hatch a plan to catch him—fast.

Ronda stared at Shay with her mouth hanging open. "Let me get this straight. This all happened since school got out?"

"I know. It's a lot."

"You think? And why do you guys think it's this Garrett guy again?"

Shay started taking off her clothes to get in the shower. "He tried to pick me up. And then later we saw him. He had Veronica with him. He knocked her out while we were in the vaults."

Ronda shook her head. "Shit. That's so creepy."

"Right? And now he's after me."

Shay felt the water and it was hot. Ronda stood staring at her blankly and handed her a towel.

"We are going to catch this bastard, Shay. Screw Levi. You, me, and Ryan need to make it happen. Shower and we got this. Nobody's messing with my *hoaloha*."

"Your what?"

"Best friend, silly."

Shay grabbed the towel from Ronda and waited for her to leave. "*Mahalo*," she said, pleased with herself she remembered how to say thank you. Ronda returned a minute later with clean shorts and a shirt. She set them on the bathroom counter.

Shay hadn't realized how dirty she'd been until the moss and muck in the bottom of the tub started to puddle. That canal was nasty. She felt like the tub looked. So many emotions rolling around inside. She was still sad about Levi. She was mad that she was sad. The idea of getting closer to Ryan made it better, although she worried about how that would influence her relationship with Ronda. To say it was complicated was an understatement.

When she finished her shower, she discovered the clothes Ronda had left. Shay wasn't one of those girls who took a long time getting ready in the morning. She let her hair dry naturally and didn't bother much about makeup. She knew some girls that took an hour and a half to get ready. That seemed like a huge waste. She threw on the clothes, dried her hair with the towel, and went in search of Ronda.

Ryan and Ronda were on separate sides of the bar in the kitchen. On the counter between them were the after school staples: peanut butter, honey, and Saltine crackers. Next to the crackers lay a whiteboard and bright Neon Dry Erase markers.

"That's better," said Ronda, patting the stool next to her and handing Shay a cracker. "Now you don't smell like dead fish."

Ryan smiled at Shay and scooped peanut butter into his mouth from the spoon. "You didn't smell bad."

"Yeah, thanks," said Shay grabbing the cracker. She hopped up on the stool and propped up her ankle on Ronda's leg.

Ryan set the peanut butter down and pushed the jar in Shay's direction.

"Here's the plan," said Ryan, clearly laying his claim as ring leader. "We stick a cell behind Dad's chair before Alex gets here. He never sits anywhere else."

"We can use mine," said Ronda, her mouth full of cracker.

"Great. We'll time it so that it gets Dad's and Alex's talk. See what they know that can help us," said Ryan.

"Okay. We get the intel. Then what?" asked Ronda, chomping.

"Then we listen for details to add to Ryan's CSI board out back."

"Ooooh, you showed her?" Ronda looked at Ryan then back at Shay. "I don't even get to go in The Shed."

"Ronda, you need to focus here," said Ryan. "People are dying—*kids* are dying."

Ronda turned to Shay, "But you've got to admit it's creepy. Is it creepy?"

Shay turned Ronda's bar stool so she was facing Ryan.

Ryan raised his voice. "Focus." He tapped his board with the marker.

In a hurry to be helpful Shay offered, "I heard Veronica was walking to the post office and that he trapped her in there and grabbed her."

"Where'd you hear that?" asked Ryan.

"Kailee. She texted." She pulled out her cell and passed it around. "See? It's right here."

"She's the gossip queen of middle school. She knows everything."

"Everybody knows everything. The question is, why don't the police know?" said Ronda. "And why aren't we telling Dad again?"

"Don't you think if they had enough evidence they'd have him by now? They have rules, protocol they have to follow." Ryan's frustration showed in his creased forehead. "Besides, Garrett's threatened Shay and her family. Do you trust Officer Dell with Shay's life?"

Dell was about three hundred pounds with a mean case of asthma. Jefferson was his territory. "You make a good point," said Ronda. The Department was not known for the quick ability to solve a case.

Ryan hit the white board with his purple marker like he was trying to hammer in his point. "Here's the key. We need to move fast. I'd like to track him tomorrow from the time he wakes up."

Shay sat up straight and leaned on the bar toward Ryan. "I know where he lives. I even know where his room is in the house if that helps."

"That's just too freakin' weird," said Ronda.

"I know."

Shay could tell Ryan was getting irritated with their side talk by the way he glared at Ronda, but he kept his cool. "Good, Shay. That's helpful."

Ronda piped in, "Hey, you should spend the night, right? I mean, so we can get up early and get going."

"Good," Ryan agreed. "But we still need Alex here so don't call yet. We'll wait until he gets here to ask."

"He'll be thrilled," mumbled Shay, cracker crumbs falling from her mouth. "He loves it when I ask to do things in front of other people." She tried to cover her mouth before Ryan saw.

"Too late," he laughed, and added, "Yep. Parents and their stupid rules."

The three continued to plot their investigation over peanut butter crackers. Finally, Ronda said, "This is exhausting. Can't we just chill for a few minutes? Watch *Dance Moms* or something?"

Ryan looked at Ronda like he was sorry they'd brought her in. "Sure. Knock yourself out."

All Shay could think about was the idea of facing Garrett again. It was a thought that horrified her.

Chapter 6

vic·tim
'viktəm/
noun
a person harmed, injured, or killed as a result of a crime, accident,
or other event or action; a person who seems himself as such.

Ronda's room was all about pink. It was much bigger than Shay's room and about ten thousand times more girly. The stand out item: a pink shag carpet with a rainbow-colored peace sign in the middle. The walls, also pink, but lighter than the shag, were accented with black shelves. Trophies from dance competitions sat proudly doing high kicks in the air. Between the shelves, framed shots of Ronda at various ages in an array of dance costumes filled every last bit of empty wall. Ronda's hair and makeup looked like she was on the beauty queen circuit. Shay had been in Ronda's room before, but this time she was jittery from the day's events. This quite possibly could have been the most erratic day of her life so far. Studying the walls distracted her from the chaos.

"How old were you here?" Shay asked, pointing to a shot of Ronda in black leggings and a half shirt done up in black sequins.

"Six," said Ronda. "We won that competition." Ronda struck the pose in the picture. She popped one knee, stuck her butt out, and pulled up her shirt showing off her toned abs.

"There it is," said Shay, admiring Ronda's belly button ring. "I can't believe your mom let you wear that much make-up."

"Honestly, I can't even remember if my mom was there. I probably went with Sylvia," said Ronda, plopping down on her bed and grabbing the remote. Sylvia was Ronda's nanny when she was younger. Ronda was the only person Shay knew in Jefferson with a nanny. "I think that's why I like *Dance Moms* so much. They may be crazy, but at least they show up."

Shay heard the hurt in Ronda's voice. She knew what that felt like, to be navigating on your own. She understood absent. She always felt her parents had something better to do. She tried not to let it bug her, but deep down, it did. For Ronda, she wondered if all the privilege didn't make up for that just a little bit. Shay was missing privilege *and* parents.

"Aren't you proud of your parents, though? They're very successful, right? The Hawaii trips?" Shay asked pointing to a shot of Ronda with a exotic bronzed Hawaiian fire dancer.

"To tell you the truth, I'd rather just have one that's here," said Ronda pointing at her big screen with the remote. "I get that I have swag and all, but I'd take just having somebody around when I got home."

"You have Ryan," said Shay and bounced on the bed next to Ronda.

"Like I said, it'd be nice to have somebody home. He's always out there in his shed," Ronda said. "I love him, but it's creepy. And he's mean."

"He's gone through a lot. That's got to be hard, losing someone like that." Shay felt her stomach tighten. She knew siblings did this sort of mental banter, but as an only child, she didn't really understand it. She would have killed to have a brother or sister. She already felt defensive of Ryan.

"Whatev. I'm so done with this day," said Ronda, staring at the screen.

Dance Moms played in the background and Shay was immediately drawn in. She laid next to Ronda, happy to be quiet, ankle elevated on a pillow that Ronda had given her, along with an ice pack. *Dance Moms* was almost over when a knock on the door startled her. Shay looked at Ronda. She was out cold. Shay gently rolled off the bed, hobbled to the door, and answered it.

Ryan's smile greeted her from the other side. "Can I come in? I want to show you what I've worked out."

Shay put her finger to her lips, closed her eyes, and tipped her head to the side. Ryan nodded and added, "Oh. The Sleeping Princess." He lowered his voice. "Come to my room so we don't wake Her Majesty."

Shay stepped quietly into the hall and closed the door. She walked into Ryan's room, a sharp contrast from Ronda's Pink Dance Kingdom. No pink shag rugs here. The only thing in front of the small bed was a laundry basket tipped on its side with clothes spilling out. Shay looked down, searching for bare carpet to walk across.

"That's why I like the shed," she said. "No laundry." Ryan patted the bed next to him. "Here, sit."

Shay worked her way around a pair of cargo shorts and sat down next to Ryan. She liked the way she felt when she was sitting next to him. She wasn't sure if it was because of his untouchable sophomore status, or because he was different than any other guy she'd ever known. She felt a shiver as the skin of his forearm brushed against hers.

Ryan pulled out Ronda's cell and slid the screen to record. He handed it to Shay.

"We stick this behind your dad's chair?" Shay asked.

"Yeah. Say something."

"Ummmm. I don't know." Shay giggled at her complete fumble. She wanted to think of something clever—not corny—but when she was around Ryan, her words jumbled, and she couldn't do either.

"Here, I got something," said Ryan, holding Shay's hand and putting the speaker in front of him like a microphone. The softness of his hand surprised her. A surge of energy ran through her and almost made her drop the phone.

"I'm sitting here with the gorgeous Shay Burke, and we are one bad-ass team."

He played it back. Hearing Ryan compliment her twice in one day was definitely a high point.

Ryan stood up. "Dad should be home any time. Let's do this."

They walked down the hallway of the Reynolds home toward the kitchen. The rooms all connected in a circle. The sitting room where Chief Scott Reynolds liked to sit with his scotch and his visitors was just on the other side. In front of them, the sight of Mr. Reynolds standing at their afternoon cracker spread startled them both.

"You're home?" said Ryan.

The chief ignored him. He was dressed in black from head to toe. His badge hung on his belt. Shay could see his resemblance to Ronda, but not Ryan.

"You remember Ronda's friend, Shay?" Ryan asked.

"Hey, Shay. How's it going?" Mr. Reynolds was wiping honey off the bar. "Ryan, forget something?" He pointed to the mess on the counter, eyebrows raised.

Ryan rolled his eyes. "Didn't hear you come in."

"Don't sound so excited. I could leave if that would be better." He let out a loud, awkward laugh. "And I didn't ask who got it out. What I asked was who is going to clean up? Oh, and I have the answer. That would be you."

Ryan's jaw tightened. He turned to Shay to see her reaction. Shay shot him a comforting glance.

"Sorry, Mr. Reynolds. We were just coming out to take care of that," said Shay.

"You let Ryan do it. One way or another, we'll make him a man," the Chief glared at a quiet Ryan and then turned back to Shay. "Are you limping?"

Ryan answered before Shay could respond. "She tripped at track. Don't worry. Ronda has her elevating with ice."

"It doesn't look like she has her elevating. Where is the Princess, anyway?" asked the chief.

"In her room asleep. We were just coming out to clean up."

Kona tore around the kitchen corner where he had been licking crumbs off the floor and ran toward Shay. She bent over to pet him, thankful for the diversion.

"Sorry about the mess," she repeated, looking up at the chief, her heart pounding.

The older man settled a bit. "Alex will be over in about an hour. I'm going to take Kona out for a quick walk. Just let Alex in if he gets here early." At the word "walk," Kona lost control and started barking.

"No," the chief yelled, louder than the situation warranted. He clipped the leash on Kona and yanked him. Kona yiped. "Sit." Kona cowered. "Now let's go." He yanked the pup and off they went. Shay watched them leave, wondering why he seemed to feel the need to bully everything and everyone.

Ryan closed the front door behind him. "Let's compare notes. Who hates their dad more?"

"You don't like yours, either?"

"Yeah, right. You saw him. He's great if you like super control-freak, never wrong kinda dudes who abuse small animals. You also get the added perks like his testosterone-crazed lifestyle of football and poker parties. Honestly, I don't even think he's my dad."

"Really?"

"No—yes—I don't know," Ryan said, heading toward his room. "Maybe I dropped out of the sky from some alien ship." He threw his hands up in the air with dramatic flair, then shook his head. "We just have absolutely zero in common. He's just taking Kona out so he can jerk him around and make him do what he wants."

Shay stood still while Ryan went to the living room, slid Ronda's phone to record, and stuck it behind the chief's chair. Half-talking to himself because the chair muffled his voice, Ryan said, "Even if they don't get here for fifteen minutes, we're still good."

Shay walked over and peered down. "It's not going to ring or vibrate, right?"

"Good thinking, but, no. We're good." Ryan straightened and rubbed his hands together, pleased with his plan. "Now, let's go out to the shop and get you some crutches."

"I don't need—"

"No shame. Besides, you should keep the weight off it until we figure out if you tore something."

"I'm sure it's just a sprain," Shay said.

"Here, hop on my back. I'll give you a ride." Ryan dropped his angry eyes and turned playful. "Come on. You can do it."

Shay held on to Ryan's shoulder and jumped. He reached back to grab her from behind and hunch her up higher in position. "Woops. Sorry." He laughed as his hands touched her butt.

"No, you're not." Shay giggled, her hands around his neck as she looked out over his shoulder.

"You're right," he said, grabbing it again on purpose. "I'm not."

Shay felt Ryan's body against hers. It was strong and solid. She could feel the muscles on his back bulging as he carried her. She could smell the shampoo from his hair. She detected a slight scent of aftershave on his neck.

"You're so light," Ryan said.

"Not really. Maybe you're just really strong," said Shay. From her angle, Shay could see Ryan's cheek puff out as he smiled.

"You know, you're the highlight of my day," said Ryan.

Shay laid her head on his shoulder and wrapped her arms tightly around him. She couldn't believe how being right here made everything else seem unimportant. "And you are hands down the best part of mine."

When they got to the shop, Ryan set Shay down gently. He turned around and put his hands on her hips. Shay could feel her stomach flutter, her legs weaken. She really liked Ryan, but she wasn't sure she was ready to kiss him. Part of her wanted to bury herself in him and never come out into the world where Veronica was dead and Garrett was on the loose. Another part knew she had to focus on that real world. Ryan stared at her, reading her eyes. Then he reached up and moved a strand of hair out of her eyes.

"I'm not going to kiss you yet because I may not be able to stop," said Ryan. "But for sure, I *am* going to kiss you at some point."

Shay's throat completely clamped down and no words came out. She looked at the ground, relief and disappointment filling the same downward-cast look. If she held Ryan's gaze any longer it felt like she might lose her soul. She knew she couldn't stare at the ground forever. When she finally looked up, she realized how cluttered the shop really was.

Dark and cool, it smelled like old dirt. Boxes were piled in stacks on top of old furniture. Spider webs covered exposed rafters. Exercise equipment used as shelves sat with boxes piled on top. Book cases packed with books, games, and other random items lined the walls.

"Look at all these books," Shay said, moving closer to check out the titles. Ryan was working on moving a pile of boxes to find the crutches he thought were behind them. With each move, more musty smell filled the air.

"Yeah, not really my thing. My parents can't seem to throw them away. We still have ones they read to me and Ronda when we were kids."

Shay ran her fingers along a shelf of picture books stopping on one. "Oh, I love this one."

"What is it?"

"*Rough Face Girl* by Rafe Martin. It's the Native version of *Cinderella*." Shay held the book up and showed Ryan, who peeked out to see it.

"Don't remember it," said Ryan. "In the fairytale world I'm more of a *Gingerbread Man* fan."

Shay nodded but didn't quite get it. Never one of her faves. She opened the book and thumbed through. Ryan yelled, "Score." He held up a crutch as if he'd struck gold, then grabbed a second and stood up, smiling at his conquest. Shay smiled back. He walked over and handed two crutches to Shay.

"Trade?" He took the book from her, closed it, and put it back on the shelf. "Know how to use these things?"

Shay stuck each in her armpit. "I'm sure I can figure it out."

"Good. Follow me."

The crutches were harder than she'd thought, but Shay managed to hobble back to the house behind Ryan. She preferred the way she'd gotten out to the shop better, but she couldn't go everywhere on Ryan's back. That's not something Scout would do. In fact, Scout wouldn't have let Ryan carry her in the first place. Shay knew she needed to be stronger, more independent, and stop leaning on boys so much. What she didn't understand was why that was so difficult for her.

As they walked in through the slider, Kona ran to greet them. "Hey, boy. How was your walk?" Ryan crouched down to scratch Kona on the head.

"Why was the front door open?" snapped his father.

Ryan stood up. "I have no idea. Did you close it all the way?" Ryan puffed out his chest.

"What kind of question is that, boy?" Chief Reynolds walked over and stood inches from Ryan's face. "Obviously *I* closed it all the way."

Ryan deflated his chest and stepped back. "Shay and I were out back getting my old crutches." Ryan pointed. "Like I said, I don't know."

Kona started to bark as Alex pulled up in the driveway. "Well, don't let it happen again." He glared at Ryan and Ryan glared back. The older man turned to Shay. "I've got to talk to Alex for about thirty minutes and then he's all yours.

Alex Steiner slammed the door on his cream-colored Cadillac and walked around the car, hand outstretched to greet Ryan's father. "Well, how's our local law enforcer on this fine May day?" Alex addressed the chief with a firm handshake and big smile.

"Doing great, Alex. How 'bout yourself?"

Alex pulled away his hand and slapped Reynolds on the back, straightening the pink dress shirt he wore over light brown slacks and dark brown dress shoes. Shay always thought he overdressed, too fancy for Jefferson. "Great? Killer on the loose and you're doing great?"

The chief grimaced as the six-foot six Alex and his extra belly stepped inside. "That *is* an issue, my friend. That is an issue."

Alex noticed Shay as he walked in and smiled, although the smile didn't quite reach his steel grey eyes, eyes that could shift from jovial to furious in a flash. "Well, hello, Shay-Shay. How was your day?"

It wasn't customary for Alex to show Shay affection in public. She was thankful for that. "Fine," she said, and then, "Is it okay with you if I stay over tonight? Ronda and I have a project for school."

Alex hated Shay asking permission in front of other people and Shay knew it. She also knew he was more likely to say yes if she did it that way. He ran his fingers through his longish, wind-tossed gray and black hair before answering. "Your mom's going over to the coast for a few days so that just leaves you and me. Well, now just me."

"Thanks, Alex." Shay tried not to show the relief she felt about not having to be home alone with him. She could feel Ryan studying her face.

Chief Reynolds turned toward Ryan and Shay. "Now we need some privacy. Maybe you can go in Ryan's room and hang out."

"Don't do anything I wouldn't do," said Alex. "That leaves everything pretty much wide open." Alex slapped the chief again and laughed a creepy laugh.

Chapter 7

ge·o·cach·ing
ˈjēōˌkaSHiNG
noun
recreational activity of hunting for and finding a hidden object by
means of GPS coordinates posted on a website.

By the time Alex and Chief Reynolds finished talking, the sun was
nearly down. They then announced they were taking their meeting
downtown to The Golden Room since their wives had abandoned them
for the night and they didn't have anything better to do besides drink
whiskey and play poker.

Ryan and Shay had used that talking time to discuss all Ryan had
learned about Julia Baird's murder and how that information might help
them catch Garrett. Ryan knew a lot more than Shay realized and he
elaborated in detail. His recount made her squirm and squeeze her legs
together tight during the most disturbing parts.

His theories struck Shay as oddly possible. Ryan had profiled Garrett
as a game player, and game in every sense of the word. He was a chess
player, lining up his moves three steps in advance. He was a hunter,
stalking his prey. He was a gamesman, displaying his kill. The fact that
Ryan got all this out of two murders disturbed and impressed Shay
simultaneously.

The most disturbing theory in a laundry list of all things disturbing
was Ryan's theory about Geocaching. Shay had never heard of it, but as
Ryan described it, Geocaching was definitely something nerds would do.
It involved latitude and longitude—Nerd Clue #1—and locating
coordinates on an app downloaded to a cell through a GPS tracker—
Nerd Clue #2. Ryan had whipped open the app to an introductory video
of a wannabe cool guy explaining how the tracker worked in uncovering
hidden treasure. The twenty-something exposed just enough ink on his
right bicep to distract from the invisible pocket protector in his plaid
shirt. The levels of difficulty determined how hard the treasure box was
to locate. Additional clues were given if the hunter was unable to locate
the box where the treasures were hidden.

The kicker was that when the hunter found the box, he was to take
something and leave something. The items were small and insignificant.
Ryan had talked about finding a travel bug and a small plastic Lego in

one. He had taken the Lego and left a small polished rock in return. Geocaching was known only to a particular segment of the population and Geocachers would have big conventions and mass treasure hunts—Nerd Clue #3—where they all looked for clues with their faces buried in their phones.

Shay loved it. She had an inexplicable urge to go find the treasure boxes immediately until Ryan told her how he'd determined the murders could be tied to Geocaching. Julia Baird's body wasn't hidden. It was, instead, *posed in* the way that the killer wanted her to be found, half in the sun and half in the shade, with the shady side of her flesh turning to a soapy consistency. Ryan told Shay he'd heard his dad discussing this on the phone and had done his own thinking about why someone might do it.

He'd said that everybody had a shadow side and that this killer was playing on that. But that wasn't the only thing. Ryan knew the locations around town where the boxes were hidden because he and Julia had gone out treasure hunting on their first date. Julia had told him about Geocaching after a classmate in AP Geography told her one Monday what he'd done on the weekend. Ryan had thought the idea sounded like a sure bet to get Julia to a private make-out location, so he hopped on board with a pocketful of polished rocks.

When Julia's body was found, Ryan remembered that there was a cache right next to that location. He drove to the spot and, sure enough, fifty feet away, under a rock with a medium-difficulty level, was a box that held a bracelet he'd given Julia. He knew then Garrett was playing a game. Ryan decided he would be the one to win and that's when he opened his CSI stand in the shed. Now, all they had to do was unravel the rules.

"Download the app." Ryan grabbed Shay's cell, searched for the app and waited. "What's your password?"

Shay hesitated.

"What? You think I'm going to steal your identity?" Ryan waited, finger ready. "What is it?"

"Ilovelevi1!," said Shay looking down at her feet.

"Oh, original," said Ryan. "Lame-sauce."

"Agreed," said Shay, barely audibly. "I'm going to have to change that."

"Good luck changing your Apple ID. It's like breaking into the Pentagon."

"Great."

Ryan opened up the app and handed the phone back to Shay. "Read this."

Shay grabbed the phone and read: Geocaching can be dangerous. But then again, so can anything you do outside. Geocache at your own risk.

She clicked "I understand" and opened the app. "Now, what?"

"Now we've got to go check these places out. Which one do you think is our best bet?" Ryan said, raising his eyebrows.

Shay knew he already had a guess. "Hmmmm. This one sounds like a creeper." Shay pointed to *Pirate Spoils the Poodles* and Ryan read the description: "Difficulty: 1.5"

"I'm having so much fun spoiling my Poodle. She doesn't know what to think about me. I open doors. I buy her flowers and gifts. I even do the dishes, laundry and clean the house just to surprise her. I hope she keeps a silly old Pirate like me. Little does she know these acts of kindness will never wear off."

Shay finished reading about the pirate, looked at Ryan, and they both scrunched their noses.

"Yeah, not feeling the pirate." Ryan dismissed *Poodles*. "You said you saw Garrett at the cemetery, right?"

Shay shuddered, remembering. "Yes."

"When you were young, were there any places you remember him talking about that he liked? Any clues as to where he might go?"

Shay thought. "He loved the lake."

"Shasta or Whiskeytown?"

"Both, but I think mostly Shasta. I remember him talking about how he wished he had a boat and could go live in one of the coves like those lawyers in town who make money off representing him."

Ryan grabbed his
shoes and put them on. "We've got to go out there."

"Now? It's dark."

"This is serious, Shay. Tomorrow's Saturday. We need to get ahead of him. You know he's out hunting right now."

Shay hesitated. It didn't feel right.

Ryan intensified his stare. "Do you want to be responsible for the next victim?" Shay shook her head. "I'll go grab Ronda's cell and we'll listen on the way. You get Ronda."

"Wait. I thought you weren't supposed to be driving anybody yet?"

"Stupid law. Nobody cares. Besides, I'm just two months out. This is too important, and I can't really ask for a permission note from my dad to go find a killer." Ryan walked out the door and barked over his shoulder, "Go get Ronda."

Shay stared after him. His reaction weirded her out. It seemed overbearing for what she'd said. Maybe she'd sounded like a baby for asking, but she just didn't want him to get in trouble. She'd heard of other teens getting pulled over and having to pay huge fines and license suspensions. She was trying to protect Ryan.

She got up and went to Ronda's room, feeling uneasy about the whole plan. Maybe they should just go to the police. Maybe she and Ryan should just head down to the Golden Room and tell Chief Reynolds and Alex what was what. Of course, they'd be completely wasted at this point so that might not be the best idea. She opened Ronda's door. The bed was empty.

"Ryan?" she yelled down the hall. Ryan came back to Ronda's room. "She's gone."

"What do you mean gone?"

"She was laying right there on the bed," said Shay.

Ryan walked into Ronda's room. He looked under her bed. "She's probably laughing her head off right now hiding in the closet or something."

They hurried through the house, opening closets and looking under beds. "Ronda! Not funny," yelled Shay. She felt her stomach get more and more nauseous as each passing moment failed to produce Ronda. She knew something was wrong.

"I think I'm going to throw up," she said to Ryan.

"You need to chill," he said.

"I guess you're right. Could she have gone over to the neighbor's house, or out back or something?"

"Let's go look."

They searched the backyard, and then Ryan stopped. "Where's Kona?"

"Maybe that's it," said Shay.

They ran into the house, where Kona's leash hung on a hook. Ryan stopped and stared at the blue and white leash that hung on the hook then turned toward Shay. "The door. You know how Dad thought it was me—"

"But wait. Kona was still with your dad," said Shay holding her stomach.

Ryan walked to the back slider and opened it. "Kona," he yelled. "Come here boy."

Kona came running across the yard from behind the shop.

"Good boy. Okay. You can go back to your nap." Ryan shut the door. He thought for a minute. "What if Garrett was in the house? You said he chased you, right?"

Shay sat down and put her face in her hands. She knew that was right. "Shit. What are we going to do?"

"We've got to call my dad," Ryan said, heading toward the house phone. Shay nodded. Ryan picked up the phone and dialed.

Shay heard a buzzing in the other room. The chief had forgotten his cell on the table next to his chair. Shay brought the cell back and held it up. "Maybe it's a sign?"

Ryan hung up and grabbed his keys from the bowl on the kitchen counter. "Okay. We've got to get out to the lake. I think I know which cache he might go to."

"How would you know that?" asked Shay before she even realized the words were coming out of her mouth.

"There's one by the swinging rope that has a lot of foot traffic. He'd like that for staging a body. We'll need flashlights. It's steep and dark."

"Do you think she's still alive?" Shay asked, wanting to fall apart but trying to stay focused.

"For now."

Chapter 8

You Tube
yoō,yə t(y)oōb/
YouTube is a website that allows users to upload and share videos
worldwide. Launched in February 2005 by three former members of
Paypal, YouTube has seen immense success, and as of March 2006
roughly 20,000 videos are uploaded daily

Shay and Ryan screeched out of the driveway in Ryan's red Toyota
truck. He'd bought the piece of junk for five hundred down at the
ballpark. From what Shay could see, he'd paid too much. The steering
wheel shook when the speed exceeded twenty. He had to crank it hard to
correct so he didn't steer into oncoming traffic down the two-lane road.

"Pull up the app. It's called something-rope," said Ryan.

Shay located Dead Man's Rope. "Head to the lake and take the first
exit."

Ryan's air conditioning consisted of windows rolled down. Shay
could smell the pastures as they drove. Sometimes the smell was
pleasant, like clover. Others, it was awful, like two thousand cows
pooped and left it. As they drove north up Interstate 5, Shay noticed how
dark it was once they passed the city lights. The air hadn't cooled down
much, but there was a dampness she didn't usually feel here in dry
northern California. Moving into the third year of drought, all the local
ranchers could talk about was rain and how they just never seemed to get
enough. She watched as clouds formed in the dark sky, toying with
tomorrow's summer storm forecast. The waning Gibbous moon peeked
through and then hid again. Patches of stars got brighter as they drove
closer to the lake.

"Crap," said Ryan. "We forgot the flashlights."

"We can just use our phones, right?" Shay slid the flashlight to bright.

Ryan smiled. "How did they survive without them in the olden
days?" He leaned over to turn the radio to a local station. "That Girl is on
Fire" crackled through the speakers. The song was quickly interrupted by
the emergency broadcast system.

The reporter announced that another young woman was reported
missing, this time from a bar on Hillcrest Drive. Hillcrest was lined with
bars, and the reporter didn't specify which one. The reporter warned
local women to be on high alert. Two murders, and now this, pointed to a

serial killer in the area. No place should be considered safe.

Shay looked at Ryan. "Are you sure this is a good idea?"

"It's a horrible idea," he said. "But it only makes it more important we get up there and stop his ass."

Shay stared at the white dotted line as it passed under the red Toyota. She nodded. She agreed with Ryan, so why did she feel like she could vomit at any minute?

"I know. You're right," she said. "I'm just scared."

Ryan reached over and touched her bare leg with his soft hand. "I know, Shay." He smiled at her and gave her leg a little squeeze. "You know I'll take care of you, right?"

Shay put her hand on top of his. "I know. It's just been such a short amount of time and he's out of control. I just ...."

"Just what?"

"I just need to talk about it a little I guess," she said.

Ryan reached over and turned the radio off. "Talk away," he said.

"I just wonder how this happens," said Shay. "I mean, how is it that one day he's playing with us in the field and the next day he's off raping and murdering?"

Ryan shook his head. "I don't know." He sped up. "It's confusing, isn't it?"

"More like disturbing," said Shay. "I think back to different things. Like when he had his motorcycle accident."

"Accident? I don't know about that," said Ryan. "He crashed?"

"Bad," said Shay. "I know because once again he was in Alex's office. He got pretty messed up."

"What happened?"

"He was coming into town on Highway Forty-four and took the turn too fast. He laid down the Harley and had to be taken to the hospital. Major head trauma. They weren't sure he was going to make it."

"Ouch."

"Yeah. I always wondered if it was another suicide attempt. He'd already tried to shoot himself in the chest and survived that. Maybe part of him was trying to put an end to his demons."

"Or maybe he just drove too fast. Donor cycles and all that," said Ryan.

"Maybe. But it took off half his nose, Alex said. He was super self-conscious about it but couldn't afford to fix it."

"So he just went around with half a nose?" Ryan asked with a smirk.

"I don't know. Alex said he stuffed it with putty and covered it with make-up. I never looked too closely because Alex said he'd go ballistic if he thought you were staring at it."

"Sounds like a drag, but a lot of people have to deal with stuff like that and don't turn into monsters," said Ryan.

"I know," said Shay. "Alex said he was never the same in the head. I mean, he was already messed up to begin with, but things got worse. That's when he ended up in Crystal Creek for flirting with some guy's girl at the fair, then stabbing the boyfriend when the dude told him to knock it off."

"Hashtag misogynist with a major screw loose," said Ryan.

"Yep. It didn't seem like that when we were young, but it definitely seems like that now."

"You know a lot about this dude. Did he ever have a girlfriend?"

"Yes. He was in love. They had a baby, I think," said Shay, trying to remember the details. "It was very on again, off again. I think he beat her up and she left or something."

"That may have saved her life," said Ryan.

"I know." Shay sat, thinking about it. Memories were filling in like dark colors in a child's coloring book scribbled outside the lines. She'd clearly kept the covers closed for the past few years. She did that with unpleasant storylines. She'd stick them in this dark chapter of her mind and close the book. There, nobody could see them, including her. "I just hate this whole thing," she said.

Ryan fumbled around in his ashtray and pulled out a porcelain container. He steered with one hand and popped the top open with the other. "Here. Maybe this'll help."

"What is it?" Shay asked.

"Peanut Butter Cookie. Got it from the weed store."

Shay could use a hit right now, just to numb the confusing feelings. What she didn't need was to get more paranoid than she already was. "That's not the one that makes you freak the hell out about everything, is it?'

"You've never had it?"

"No."

Ryan paused. "Have you ever smoked?"

"Not really," said Shay, fumbling with the ceramic cigarette and trying to figure out how the whole thing worked.

"What's that mean, not really?"

"Well, Levi had some one time and I took a little hit, but it just made me cough so I stopped." Shay fumbled around with the container. "It definitely made me paranoid."

"Best of the North State, right here. This one will just chill you out."

"Funny name. How do you get it?"

"I have a script."

"For what?" asked Shay.

"For Peanut Butter Cookies and what the hell ever else." Ryan laughed.

Shay could tell Ryan wasn't going to elaborate, and it really didn't matter. The important thing was this could probably take the edge off a pretty horrible day that was about to get even more horrible. Ryan talked her through how to use the cigarette.

"Take that end and stick it in the hole on the top, then turn it," he said flirtatiously.

"Like this?" asked Shay, with a little smile.

"Ooooh, yeah. Just like that," he said. "Now, reach in the door and there's a lighter."

Shay reached down in the side of the door and felt around. She felt a crumpled up wrapper, a pack of gum, a ball point pen, and finally, the lighter. She pulled it out and showed Ryan.

"Good," he said. "Now, when you light the end with the bud, inhale on the other side. Just breathe deep."

Shay felt a shiver. She lit the cigarette. She didn't want to look like a beginner. She was very aware of Ryan watching her. She could feel the heat from the bright orange end as it got brighter. The smoke burned the back of her throat. She tilted her head back, held her breath, and then blew out the smoke.

The smell was strong, unlike anything else she could think of. It smelled a little like one of the skunks on the road after it'd been smashed. "Like that?" she asked.

"Exactly. Now, do it again, then refill it."

Shay didn't feel anything, so she reloaded and lit the cigarette again. As she exhaled, she started to feel dizzy.

"You okay?" said Ryan, noticing.

"A little lightheaded." It was hard to get the words out. She felt like her brain knew what it wanted to say but wasn't cooperating with her mouth. "Want some?"

"When we get there," said Ryan.

Shay wished she hadn't taken that second hit. Everything was spinning. She felt a freak-out coming on. She took a deep breath and laid her head out the window to feel the cool breeze. The air felt good on her face. She pulled her head back in and had the most awful sensation. Her face felt like it was melting. She reached her hand up and patted her cheeks. They felt normal to her hands, but from behind her face, she felt like her skin was falling off.

"I think you're high," said Ryan.

"I thought it was supposed to feel good," said Shay. "I feel like my face is dripping off."

"That's a new one," said Ryan, laughing.

Shay didn't think it was funny. She felt like crying. All she wanted to do was take the edge off her anxiety, and now she had more than ever. She looked out the window. On the side of the road, she saw bears running alongside the field.

"Oh, my God! Did you see that?"

"See what?" asked Ryan.

"Those bears! There must be ten of them."

Ryan looked into the field. "Nope. No bears, Shay. We're almost to the lake. Just sit back and close those eyes. It's all good."

Shay laid her head back and closed her eyes. The spinning motion made her feel like she was going to puke. She tried to breathe, but it was too strong. "Pull over!"

"Can't you wait? We're almost there."

"No." Shay started to heave, and Ryan screeched to a stop in the gravel off the highway.

"Okay, okay," he said. "Not in the truck." He leaned over Shay and opened the door.

For the next ten minutes, Shay hung out of the truck, vomiting on the side of the road. She wasn't sure what was making her puke. The last thing she felt like doing was going to track down Garrett, but she felt she couldn't turn her back on Ronda. She took a deep breath of the night air and sat back in the car.

"You all right?" Ryan asked. Shay detected more frustration than caring.

"Yeah." Shay reached in the side of the door for a piece of gum to erase the vomit taste.

They rode the rest of the way in silence. As they approached the lake, Ryan took the first exit past the lake. Shay navigated him to the cache, though she was having a difficult time with directional arrows that appeared to be dancing. "It looks like there's a parking lot down the hill and to the right," she said.

"Yeah," said Ryan, nodding. "I'm remembering this place. I think I used to go down here with Ronda when we were kids."

Ryan pulled the truck slowly down the curvy road and started to veer right. He stopped so abruptly Shay jerked forward. "Shit." Ryan slammed off his lights and stopped the truck.

"Drive much?" said Shay, looking up from her screen, and then, "Oh. Shit."

In the far corner sat Garret's pale-yellow Plymouth. They couldn't see anybody inside, but both Shay and Ryan slid down in the truck and peered over the dash. They stared at the car. They stared at each other. "He could have heard us coming down the hill. He's probably hiding. Here's what we do," whispered Ryan.

Immediately Shay felt better. Ryan had a plan she was confident he could pull off just by his voice. She took a deep breath.

"You head for those trees. Follow the Geocache directions to the rope."

"And you'll follow?"

"No. We need to separate."

"Separate?" Shay felt like a tractor wheel was rolling over her chest and suffocating her. "I can barely walk."

"We've got to do it this way. I'll go over and make sure he's not in the car. We'll meet back here in ten minutes. If you see anything, document it," said Ryan. "Got it?"

"That's a horrible plan." Shay couldn't feel her legs. Freak-out in session.

Ryan shook his head. "If we're together, he'll get us both."

"Yes, but …." Shay thought she was going to vomit again, but she was pretty sure nothing was left inside.

"We don't have time to argue, Shay. Just breathe." Ryan laid a hand on her back and put his face close to hers. "You got this."

Shay nodded, her head swirling. His plan reeked, but there was no time to hesitate. They needed to do this. They needed to record him in the act. She needed to suck it up and channel her inner Scout.

"Good. Lay low, though, because you know he always has knives. Mostly like a gun. And look out if he grabs a rock." Ryan opened the door slowly. "YOLO," he whispered.

Shay wasn't sure that was true. She was pretty sure you lived more than once and what you did in this lifetime would matter in the next. It made her mission to bust Garrett all that more meaningful. "We'll debate that later," she said, and waved him off.

Ryan slinked along a row of evergreens that lined the lake. Shay spotted the bridge in the distance. Every so often a car sped across and made it a few shades brighter for a split second. The clouds shifted in the gentle breeze opening up the starry night. Ripples of light danced in the dark across the water. Shay would have to depend on that light to make it to Dead Man's Rope.

Her mission now was to get out of the truck. She opened the door and crouched down. The door was heavy. She pushed it gently until it latched. Up the evergreen-covered hill she hobbled. She could smell the musty forest mixed with pine. Poky branches swiped her cheek as she pushed through. Halfway up she opened the app to figure out where she was going. The brightness from her cell lit up the entire area. She quickly turned off the screen. Garrett would hunt her out in half a second. She needed to be smart about this. She'd need to feel her way there. She'd need to use her intuition.

As she hurried up the hill, leaves crunched beneath her feet. Limbs blocked her way. Her eyes scanned the darkness for signs of Garrett. The light from the stars she was counting on to help was dimmed by towering pines. Coyotes howled. They sounded closer than Shay would have liked. Shay turned to look back down the hill. The bridge was no longer in sight.

She stood still. A snap behind her made her jerk her head around and her heart slam against her rib cage. Shivers rippled up her arms. Standing where she was, she was toast. She needed to get to the cache fast and meet up with Ryan. At the top of the hill she turned left, then stopped. More sounds. A mountain lion screamed in the distance. Faint music, probably from a houseboat miles out. Sound traveled and echoed out here in weird ways. She scanned the hill and gasped. In front of her were two glowing eyes close to the ground. She picked up a stick and threw it. The coyote turned and ran.

As she moved close to the rope, Shay thought she heard a cracking noise. Up ahead, she spotted a grove of manzanita. She crept toward it, crouched behind the huddled bushes, and tried to squint through twisty red trunks filled with pink, sticky flowers. From her vantage point, she felt she could make out the cracking noise in front of her if she held very still.

It was Garrett. His back was toward her, but it was definitely him. He was hunched over a body. She could see a girl's leg sticking out. This was the proof they needed. She shielded her phone's light with her shirt and turned on video record. Even on dim it lit up the dark forest. Shay's hands shook as she held her phone with one hand and shielded the light with her other. She saw blonde hair flung all over crunched leaves. Garrett was blocking her face, but his arm was moving. Shay couldn't figure out what he was doing. Whatever it was, he was transfixed. That was good for her because he was not focused on what was behind him.

Shay knew her phone was almost dead. She only had one bar out here; she'd have to upload later. She hit end on the record button. She hoped it worked.

Garrett stood up. He was holding something in each hand. He studied the girl. A car sped by on the distant bridge, lighting him just enough so Shay could see two large, wet, red hands. One held a long-bladed knife. She couldn't make out the other shape.

Shay shoved her cell in her pocket. The girl was clearly still being staged and she'd captured that. At least it wasn't Ronda. There still might be time to save her. Garrett had a pattern of killing, holding, posing, and hunting again. There was no way to know how long between the hunting and the killing.

It'd been longer than ten minutes. Shay needed to get back for Ryan. She backed away from the thick bundles of manzanita and moved toward the path. Behind her, she heard a stick snap in half. She froze. She looked at Garrett, who jerked his head in her direction. The hunter and the hunted. Shay's heart pounded so loud she was certain he could hear it.

Garrett walked toward her, eyes crazed with the same look she'd seen at the cemetery. They were hollow and detached, like someone—some *thing*—had taken over his body. Shay didn't think she could get away fast enough in her condition. Even if she started now and limped down the hill, he'd catch her. She held her breath. He moved closer. The eerie sound of his laughter shattered the forest's quiet.

"What the hell took you so long?" he said.

Shay heard a smack, felt a sharp pain on the side of her head, and dropped to the ground.

Chapter 9

Global Positioning System (GPS)
(glō'bəl *puh*-**zish**-*uh* n-een **sis**-*tuh* m)
noun
a system of earth-
orbiting satellites, transmitting signals continuously
toward the earth, that enables the position of a receiving device on or
near the earth's surface to be accurately estimated as to
location and time

When Shay came to, her hands and feet were bound tight. She wasn't sure with what. Her eyes and mouth were both covered, making it hard to breathe. She was jammed between two objects. Behind her, sticky flesh that wasn't hers pressed up against her bare legs. She squirmed against it, but it wasn't moving. *Breathe,* she told herself. *Fill up your belly and breathe. In. Out.* She inhaled and breathed into her belly as deeply as she could. The air smelled like dust and made her choke.

After her lungs settled down, Shay realized her head was throbbing. She'd had concussions before, and this felt like another. They usually made her throw up. Forget the dust. If she puked, she'd choke right here in the dark on her own vomit. She tried not to think about it so it would pass.

Beneath her, the surface rattled. It felt as if she was being driven down a dirt road with huge potholes every twenty feet. When he hit one, Shay's head slammed against the floor, which made the pain worse. The air was hot and wet. She could hear rock music blaring. The car dropped to an angle like it was going downhill. They switched back and forth, turning sharply. Shay got carsick when she sat in the front seat on roads like this. With each turn, her body pressed into the other hot body spooning her from behind. She tried to pull away, but the incline pushed her back. She gave in and relaxed into the fleshy mound. The body was bigger in size and had hairy legs.

Gravel spit out from the tires as the car skidded to a halt. Shay heard the music stop and the car door slam. She froze. The trunk popped open. She faked sleep.

"Well, isn't that a pretty picture?" Shay heard Garrett say. "Two little love birds, sitting in a trunk." Ryan. Ryan was in here with her. Garrett laughed. "Bet you didn't think your first date would look like this."

When neither of them moved, Garrett reached in and grabbed Shay around the middle. She tried to make herself as limp and heavy as possible. Dead weight without the dead part. He heaved her over his shoulder and started walking downhill. With her eyes and mouth covered, she had to rely on smell and sound. Water lapped against the shore. Wet earth and fish smell filled the air. She wondered if Garrett was going to throw her in. The water was still cold from the snow melt off Mt. Shasta. She'd freeze in ten minutes.

Garrett walked into the water, making sloshing sounds as he moved along the shallow shoreline. Shay held her breath, ready to drop into the dark cold. She'd heard drowning was not a great way to go. Given Garrett's recent history, though, it might be the best of all options. At least maybe this way she'd have the opportunity to figure out some Houdini move beneath the water and swim away — if she didn't freeze first.

Garrett heaved her off his shoulder and dropped her down with a thud. She fell against a cold, rough surface. Garrett sloshed back through the water. Shay lay there alone. Her body rocked to and fro with the water. She was on a boat, but she wasn't sure what kind. She tried to imagine what the boat was like. She squirmed to see if she could feel anything with her bound hands. The bottom was rough and kept her from moving very far. She was also keenly aware that if she wiggled too much in one direction, she might go flying off the boat into the water.

The water sloshed again, followed by another loud thud. Garrett had returned with the other body which he plunked down next to Shay. Shay heard a muffled moan.

"Don't make me double-tape you there, cowboy," said Garrett. "Don't want to waste my tape. This stuff comes in handy." He laughed.

Shay listened closely. Garrett pushed the boat off the shore and hopped on. The sound of the motor told Shay they were probably on a patio boat. She'd been coming to the lake since before she could walk, and had learned about all different types of boats over the years. This one was low and quiet, not like a speed boat or a houseboat. The sound of water lapping against the boat made her suddenly aware of how bad she had to pee.

As they moved across the lake, Garrett hummed. Shay needed to get his attention, or she was going to pee all over herself. She kicked her legs and heaved her chest forward. When she did that, she knocked into a pole that fell over and clanged against the boat.

"Cool it," he yelled.

Shay continued. Garrett turned off the motor and walked over to Shay. She felt his shoe on her chest. "You deaf? I said 'knock it off.'" He leaned down toward Shay's face. Shay tried to yell "pee" under her tape, but it just came out like "eeeee".

"Just for old times, Shay, I'm going to pull back this tape. So help me God if you scream, nobody will hear you, and I promise I will kick your ass overboard into this lake and leave you for dead."

Shay nodded.

Garrett reached behind her head and untied the blindfold. He smiled at her with wild blue eyes. His brown wispy hair hung down in his face. Even though Garrett's face was terrifying, it felt good to open her eyes. Garrett gently moved her hair out of her face. Shay stared up at him and wondered how he'd done the things he'd done. In the dark, with the stars backlighting him just enough to see his features, Shay remembered what made her like him when she was young. His high cheekbones and a strong jawline were stunning. He had a dimple in his chin which softened his look. His lips were full, his skin tanned and clean shaven. His most striking feature was his eyes. They were icy blue, but it was the way they penetrated Shay's soul that made her feel their intensity. Beyond his looks lay an indescribable charm. Shay couldn't put it into words. She had seen what he was capable of with Veronica and Julia. She couldn't reconcile that with the face she was seeing and the emotions she was feeling. All she knew was she wanted to please him.

He put his finger in front of his lips. "Remember."

Shay nodded again. She wasn't going to scream.

Gently, he pulled the tape from her lips. "Sorry I had to do that, Shay, but you were trying to ruin my work." He stared at her and smiled. "Now, what's the issue?"

Shay squeezed her legs together. "I really need to pee," Shay whispered. "I don't want to go all over myself."

Garrett, still bending down next to Shay, traced his finger along her hairline. "Such a beautiful face. You know I always liked you best."

Shay felt her face get hot and her stomach knot. "Really?"

"Really. Let me get you un-taped and you can go off the side of the boat." Garrett pulled her to a seated position and began untying her hands. "Just don't get any ideas"

Shay shuddered. "I won't," she said. "I promise."

Once Shay sat up, she was able to look around the boat. The patio boat was large with a big flat surface and green benches on the sides. There was a cover on top that was pulled back, opening to the sky. The wheel and captain's chair were up at the right and a passenger chair was next to it. Lying on the ground was Ryan. Blood covered his cheek.

Garrett freed her hands and Shay shook them out. She felt her pocket. No cell. Her shoulders hurt from having them in that position so long. She still felt queasy from the crack to the head, and her head throbbed. Garrett used his knife to cut the tape on her feet.

"Is he going to be okay?" said Shay, pointing at Ryan.

"You mean your new little boyfriend? Didn't you just have a different one yesterday?"

"Long story. He's just a friend."

"Oh, really? How well do you know him?"

Shay suddenly felt like she was chatting with one of her classmates in Chem over Bunsen burners. "How well do you know him?" *How well do you know anybody?* She needed to pee like yesterday.

"Not well. Ummm, how should I do this? I'm still a little dizzy from the—well, you know."

Garrett helped Shay up and scanned the boat. The slight wind was pushing them toward the opposite shore even without the motor running. "How about you hold on to that bar and drop your ass over the side? Can you do that?"

Shay wasn't sure she was strong enough in her current state, but she was willing to try anything at this point. "Sure. I can do it." She moved to the side, grateful to have her feet back. Garrett watched her.

"Would you mind?" she asked. "I can't go while you're watching."

"Oh, sure." Garrett turned the opposite way. "Sorry."

Shay held onto the side bar and dropped her ass toward the water. Garrett hummed as she peed. The water wasn't as cold as she'd thought. She could just drop into it and swim like crazy underneath like she had in the canals. It was dark enough for her to hide along the shore. She couldn't do that to Ryan though. Or Ronda.

"Finished?" Garrett asked, interrupting her escape plan and still looking away.

"So much better. Thanks," she said. She shook, stepped up, and pulled up her shorts.

"No prob. Why don't you have a seat up here with me."

Shay looked at Ryan and then at the seat. "Yeah, okay." She looked over at Ryan. "Is he hurt?" she asked, trying to sound disinterested.

"Nah. Just a little sleepy juice. He'll be fine."

Shay moved to the passenger seat. Garrett started up the boat.

"Where we going?"

"It's a surprise."

Shay loved surprises, but not of this kind. Garrett sat back and steered the boat with one hand. "Nice night, huh?" He looked at her like they were on a date.

"Beautiful."

And it was. The night lake was a magical place. The clouds pushed back on either side and the sky was soaked in stars. The tall evergreens hugged the shores of Shasta Lake, allowing for small sandy beaches in scattered places, private places for lovers at midnight. Shay could lay for hours and look at the stars, making pictures in the sky. May was early for the houseboat travelers that would come in droves in June. Tonight, they were completely alone.

"Just past the full moon," said Garrett. "Such symbol of knowing, of intuition."

Shay turned to see Garrett's eyes turned toward the sky. He was another man in that moment. A poet. An artist. Sensitive to the landscape and nature. Serial killer turned Transcendentalist. The contrast was incredibly weird.

"I never really thought about that," said Shay. "By the way, do you have my cell?" Shay said, brushing his arm with her hand. Shay was a survivor. She'd had practice putting up with what others needed in order to get what she needed. Alex's late night, whiskey-drenched visits had taught her that.

Garrett continued to gaze upward, ignoring her. "It's important, the moon cycles. Pay attention to those. Knowing them can help you guide your life."

Shay was used to being ignored, too. She looked out at the water glistening under the stars. She looked back up at the crescent. She wondered if Garrett realized she'd taped him and had her phone or if he'd just left it in the forest by the hanging rope. "How so?"

"Well, it's the only natural satellite of the Earth, for one. If the moon affects the tides of the ocean with its gravitation, doesn't it make sense it would also affect you?"

Shay was fascinated by this bizarre misplaced conversation on astronomy. She knew what Garrett needed. New moon, new ideas and all. Sitting here, gazing at the stars, it was easy to remember why she'd been smitten by this killer once upon a time. He was charming. It was easy to see how he could get women to come with him wherever he wanted to take them.

"Yeah, I guess it does," said Shay, smiling at him. She reached over and touched his hand. "What are all those things moving up there?"

Garrett looked at her hand touching his, then at Shay. The edges of his lips turned up slightly and his blue eyes twinkled in the starlight. He held that gaze a moment before returning his eyes to the sky. "Those are the other kind of satellites. They're the ones that make your GPS work."

Hundreds of bright lights moved about the sky. "That's crazy," said Shay. "I had no idea."

"More and more each day," said Garrett. "I like to lie out here all night and look up at them, imagining what it would be like to be up there. Away from this shit-hole of a place."

Shay sensed his mood shift and wanted to get him back on star happy. "I guess I'll learn more about them. We haven't studied them in school yet."

"School. They teach you a bunch of shit nobody cares about. Never liked it."

Shay knew better than to argue, but she disagreed. She liked school. She did know a lot of people who didn't, though. Garrett was the kind of kid the teachers picked on. He was also the kind of kid the students picked on. She understood. That colored his thoughts about it. She knew that right now he needed her to agree.

"Tell me about it. Just one long line of boring days strung together." Her head was still pounding from earlier and she felt loopy. She wondered if she'd remember any of this in the morning—if she made it to morning.

"I learn everything I need to know from my art," said Garrett.

Shay didn't remember Wayne being an artist. She did remember the blacksmith shop next to the daycare where he and Daddy Dan used to get in fist fights while The Daycare Kids stood on the black wrought iron fence and cheered them on. They'd pick sides and bet who was going to win. They'd yell, "Fight, fight, fight!" Shay was only five. She remembered being confused about whether they were fighting or playing until Wayne stood up and she saw blood on his face and the pain in his heart as he cussed at his father.

"You do art?"

"Of course. It's my passion."

"What kind of art?" Shay didn't take art classes in school anymore. Friday art flew out the window with budget cuts. She was sad when that happened back in third grade. It was always something she looked forward to.

"Do you want to see, curious girl?" Garrett asked, raising his eyebrows.

"Of course." Back to bonding. She could appeal to this sensitive side of Garrett and convince him to stop the murders, beginning with her own, Ryan's, and Ronda's if she was still alive.

Garrett reached into a black backpack down by his feet and pulled out an iPad. He flipped it on. "You sure?"

Shay hopped off her seat and moved over to look. "Of course."

The iPad opened the picture file. Garrett tapped on an icon. Up came Julia Baird, positioned in the grove of poppies, half in the sun and half in the shade.

Shay gasped and put her hand over her mouth.

"I know," said Garrett, smiling. "Good stuff, right?"

No, not good stuff! Shay pulled her words out. "Wow. I don't know what to say."

"Not an art critic, right? That's okay. A lot of thought goes into these, you know. Planning and patience. It requires originality."

Shay's mind was swirling. She had to come up with something. "Do you have any more?"

"Oh, I have lots."

Lots? Shay only knew about two. She couldn't go in too hot or Garrett would shut down. She sensed that. She'd have to enter the side door on this.

"When did you start with your art?" asked Shay, as nonchalantly as she could muster.

"Remember Sox?"

"The barn cat? The one that ran away?"

Garrett laughed, "Well, not exactly ran away. She was my first masterpiece."

"You killed Sox?" Tears backed up in her throat and she tasted the salt mixed with disgust.

Garrett's face changed. "Killed? I didn't *kill* her. I saved her."

Shay held her stomach. She felt vomit halfway up her esophagus. She'd loved Sox. "Saved her ... by—"

"You're young, Shay. You don't get it. Living is the nightmare. Dying is the good part. You just got to do it right. Make it count."

Shay didn't know what to say. He was demented. She'd definitely had dark days where she wondered if she'd be better off dead. She'd had problems she felt were too tall to scale. But she'd never thought about killing anybody, especially Sox. The weirdest part was that had this conversation, this moonlit boat ride across Shasta, taken place outside this disturbing dynamic, it would have been the best date Shay had ever been on. The fact that she even thought that made her wonder what the hell was wrong with her. *How damaged am I?* Scout never would have had a thought like that. But then again, she was only six or something and had Atticus for a dad. Shay had Alex.

"You're not saying anything." Garret scowled and looked toward shore.

"I don't know what to say." Shay didn't want to piss Garrett off, but she hated what he was saying. She could feel herself walking the tight rope between bonding and death. She needed to stick on the bonding side. "I've never thought about death the way you're describing it."

"Basically, I just wanted to make a difference. I want to mean something. To leave a legacy behind." Garrett paused and looked pensively toward the shore. "This world is a twisted load of crap and I just want to do something beautiful."

Shay thought about his words and tried to ignore the fact that his *something beautiful* was what was completely twisted. "I get that. I think we all want that." She felt him warming. "Can I ask you something?"

"Sure, Shay. I like talking to you. I don't remember the last time I had a real conversation with anybody. I might just keep you around for a while."

Shay felt sad for him, but also disturbingly flattered and relieved. "When did you get the idea for the geocache boxes? So clever."

Garrett laughed. "Sort of by chance." He looked at Shay. "I was inspired."

"By what?"

"By The Daycare Kids," he said.

Shay felt her stomach drop, afraid of what he'd say next. "What happened?"

"Well, you know I never liked The Daycare Kids."

"You acted like you did."

"Because if I didn't, Dad beat me with the belt."

"I think I remember hearing that," said Shay.

"Yeah, it was a hundred times worse after you left. I couldn't even walk when he was done."

"That must have been so awful," she said, studying his empty eyes.

Garrett turned away. "That was a long time ago. All they did was take my mom's attention away so that she had none at the end of the day for me. Then, when Dad kicked the shit out of me, they stood on the fence and cheered. Remember that, Shay?"

Shay did remember. "Yeah." She didn't like where this was going.

"You remember. You were one of them."

Shay gazed across the water. Garrett changed gears faster than anybody she'd ever met. One minute he was sad, then angry, then poetic, then sweet. It was mind boggling. They were moving closer and closer to the opposite shore of the lake. She thought she made out a boating dock under the starlight. She knew she needed to say something.

"I hated that, personally. But it was confusing. We were so young and on some level we didn't realize you were fighting for real. At least, many of the kids didn't."

Garrett stood up and his eyes flashed. "*Didn't realize*? Didn't realize that my dad was kicking the shit out of me?"

Ryan stirred on the deck.

Shay needed to diffuse the situation. "Sorry, Wayne. That must have been so embarrassing for you."

He sat back down and put his hands on the wheels. "I was young, too," he said quietly.

They sat in silence for a few minutes and then Garrett changed the subject. "You asked about the geocaching. I was watching The Daycare Kids find Easter eggs and I had this thought: wouldn't it be funny if they found a finger in one of the eggs?" He laughed, a deep belly laugh that sent chills up Shay's spine. "Well, wouldn't it?"

"It would terrify them, that's for sure," said Shay.

"Like they did me when they bet that Dad would beat me to death? You do know I realized that was happening, right?"

Shay shook her head in silence.

Garrett paused and took a breath. "Anyway, the geocaching was a way I could insure people would see my art. It'd be a shame to go through all that work and not have at least somebody see it, right?"

"I see your point." Shay couldn't play this charade any longer. She knew Garrett had a gun; she'd seen it. She was a good swimmer. She also knew she had to save her friends. "What do you have planned for me?" she asked finally.

"Something very, very special, Shay," he said, looking back at Ryan. "You're going to love it."

Shay looked down at his feet. "Oh, my God! What's that?"

"I don't see anything," he said.

"I think it's a snake," she said.

Garrett bent down to look under the bow of the boat. "It crawled that way." Shay pointed forward.

Garrett got down on his hands and knees and looked. Shay grabbed the pole that had fallen. Her hands were shaking. She held it toward the reel and smacked Garrett hard over the back of the head. She turned and jumped off the side of the boat and heard Garrett scream, "You bitch!" as her body hit the freezing water.

Chapter 10

Fish Finder
. (fish fin-dər)
noun
Uses traditional yet effective wired function to detect the
schools of fish in any particular area and depth of water

The water hit Shay like a block of ice. The shock of temperature change cut her breath in half. Black engulfed her. She was back swimming in the canals all over again. The goal was to stay far enough below surface so Garrett couldn't see the motion she made. He'd shoot her. Down too deep, and she'd get disoriented. Balance was the key.

She squeezed her eyes shut and swam as far from the boat as she could. She had no idea where she was going. She just knew her life depended on getting away. She'd have to feel her way. The water felt silky through her fingers as she dragged them, stroke after stroke, through the water. Her younger years swimming for the Gators swim team was paying off. Those two-a-day practices might be just what saved her life. If she could get far enough away from Garrett, she could take a quick breath and hope he was looking the opposite direction at the time. Once she got to shore, she could make her way up under the bridge to the highway and flag someone down.

At some point, the cold no longer gripped her arms and legs. Either she was numb or shot up with adrenaline. She didn't care. Slimy lake plants stretched up from the lake bottom and licked her legs as she frog-kicked through. Her inner thighs burned. She needed air. Her head started to feel light. She'd have to take a breath soon. She flipped around to look toward where she thought the boat would be. She tried to come up quietly. When she did, she gasped. Garrett was in the water swimming toward her.

She turned and sprinted as fast as she could toward the shore. She could hear him yelling in her direction. Her heart pounded in her ears. Her lungs burned.

"I'm coming for you, you little bitch," he yelled.

Garrett swam fast behind her. Shay switched to freestyle. She kicked as hard as she could, but she could hear Garrett gaining. His feet slapped the water violently. She hadn't taken him for such a swimmer. Each stroke made Shay's arms more tired. There was no way she could keep up her current pace. As she kicked her feet, she felt something grab one. She tried to kick it off, to release the grasp, but her legs were too tired. It pulled her under the water. The surprise left her no time to gasp for air. She choked on the lake water. She flailed her arms. She kicked her legs. Still the hand held her down.

In a moment, everything shifted. She felt the energy leave her body. She felt limp. It felt good to let go, to surrender to whatever happened. She floated up to the surface with her eyes closed. As her face broke the surface, she gasped. Garrett had his arm around her neck in a rescue hold. He was paddling the water with one arm and cursing under his breath as he went. Shay was somewhere between wakefulness and sleep, lying on her back with her head floating on the water.

As he approached the boat, Garrett mumbled something about getting back on it. He wrapped his hand through Shay's hair and yanked hard. Stabbing sensations shot through her head. He heaved himself up on the side of the boat, then pulled Shay up by her hair. She cried out. Garrett grabbed one arm with the other hand and lifted her from the water. He rolled her onto the boat bottom and straddled her, putting his face right up to hers.

"Don't *ever* try that again." He spit as he said it, eyes flashing. "It's not like you're going to get away. Haven't you ever heard of fish finder?"

Shay hadn't even thought about him being able to track her under the water. He stood up and walked to the captain's chair. A rustling noise told Shay he was grabbing something. He returned with a towel and his tape. He threw the towel at Shay.

"Dry off," he said. "I'm disappointed in you, Shay."

Shay sat up and dried her body. He was angrier than she'd ever seen him. "I thought we understood each other better." He pulled out his tape and bent down to wrap Shay's wrist and mouth. "Now I can't trust you."

After he finished, he used a rope to tie Shay to the side of the boat.

Chapter 11

cav·ern
ˈkavərn/
Noun
The cave you fear to enter holds the treasure you seek.
~Joseph Campbell

The boat pulled up to the dock and Garrett helped Shay off with a warning that if she tried anything again, he'd have to shoot her in the foot, then peel her skin off and make a winter coat out of it. He promised to do that while she was still alive. Shay didn't doubt he was telling the truth. He grabbed a bag from under the bow and threw his iPad inside. He grabbed still-groggy Ryan and flung him over his shoulder.

He motioned to Shay. "After you."

Shay stepped off the boat and onto the rocky shore. Garrett tied the rope around a metal stake jutting out of the water. "Here, loop this through," he said to Shay.

Shay reached over, grabbed the end of the rope and stuck the end through the hole. She'd learned about knots in boat camp, but her mind was blank right now. Garrett stared at her. She needed his help, but he was clearly irritated about having to give it. If the boat didn't stay anchored, she wasn't sure how they'd ever get away. The width was too far to swim.

"I'm not sure how," said Shay.

"You don't know how to tie a damn knot?"

"I forget."

He flung Ryan to the ground, grabbed the rope from her, and with a condescending tone said, "You really need to learn the most basic of all basics, Shay. How did you even get by in the world?"

Shay looked down. He reminded her of Alex. He always had to put her down to feel good about himself. She knew what he was doing, but it still hurt her feelings. Ryan squirmed on the ground, which made her feel even worse. Garrett followed her eyes down to Ryan.

"That's your fault. I wouldn't have had to throw him in the dirt if you could have done the most basic task of tying a knot, now would I?" He hiked Ryan up on his shoulder and said, "Follow me."

Shay hated him. She hated what he stood for, what he'd done to others, what he'd done to her. She didn't care why he was the way he was anymore. She imagined him going through the same thing he put everyone else through. She was sick with herself that she'd ever thought he was anything more than a monster. He was mean and demented, and she wished he was dead.

They scaled the rocky shore, crossing through a grove of tall pines which opened into a steep mountain of gray rock. Granite, Shay thought it was. When they reached the side of the mountain, Garrett plopped Ryan on the ground. Ryan let out a moan and said, "Dude." Shay looked down at him and felt her heart lighten. She was happy he was still breathing.

The mountain had a hole in it that looked big enough to crawl through, but the hole was blocked with a boulder and some brush. Garrett cleared the brush with his hands. He kneeled down and grabbed the boulder, muscles popping in all directions. Beads of sweat covered his shoulders. He grunted. "A little help?" he asked, looking at Shay like he was annoyed she hadn't offered.

Shay didn't want to, but she knew she had no choice. She moved toward the huge rock to help. Together, they pushed the boulder back just enough to get in. Garrett stood up and looked at Ryan. "Can you walk yet, or do I still need to carry your ass?"

Ryan looked down at his feet. "Untie these and I can."

Garrett untied Ryan's feet and pushed him into the hole, kicking him. Shay followed. Garrett crawled in last, leaving the boulder ajar. He reached through the opening to the outside and pulled over enough shrubbery to camouflage. Shay was pretty sure nobody came out here anyway. The caverns that people visited on tours were a half mile toward the bridge through treacherous rock.

On the other side of the hole was a small tunnel, tight on all sides. The only way through was to drop down on hands and knees and crawl.

"Hurry up. Go," said Garrett, staring at Shay and Ryan. Ryan still seemed out of it. Shay was terrified of small spaces and thought she might have a freak-out and die halfway in.

"It's pitch black in here," said Shay, squatting down to peek into the tunnel. "How are we supposed to see?" She felt around the sides of the tunnel with her hand. The ground was cold and damp. The sides and top of the tunnel felt slippery.

"Just crawl," said Garrett. "Or I can just kill you right here." He waved his gun at them.

"We're going," said Ryan. "Go ahead, Shay. I'll follow you."

Garrett lagged behind. "Good choice. I've got to take care of something. I'll be there in a minute."

"Wait," said Shay. "Where are we going?"

"You'll know when you get there." Garrett laughed.

The feeling of moving through darkness without any idea of what was on the other side terrified Shay. Ryan sensed her fear and rubbed her lower back.

"It's okay, Shay. I'm right here with you," he said, kneeling down to hands and knees and waiting for her to do the same.

Shay kneeled and started to crawl. The silence in the mountain was deafening. It was as if they were crawling into the center of the earth. Shay swore she could hear the blood pumping through her veins. She could hear Ryan's heartbeat. She could hear them breathing in unison. Even the quietest noise echoed off the tunnel walls. Shay had never heard silence like that. Even on the quietest days, there was the buzz of her cell signaling a text every few minutes. She kept squeezing her eyes shut rather than opening them wide, thinking they would adjust to the dark. They didn't. All she could see was pitch black. The cool air felt nice after the hot day, but that niceness was countered by the crest of the freak-out she was riding. At any moment, she might lose it completely.

She tried to shift her thoughts. *Think of it as an adventure. Pretend you're Scout heading up to Boo Radley's house.* That helped for a minute. Ryan crawled close behind. Garrett had left on Ryan's hand ties, which made him move slowly. Shay could hear each hand hit the ground.

"Shit." Ryan stopped. "Moving on all fours is harder when it's just three."

Shay wriggled her body to face his. The tunnel was barely wide enough to turn around. "You okay?"

"Hold still," Ryan said.

"What's wrong?" Shay asked.

Ryan waited for a few moments and then said, "Shhh. Don't say anything."

Shay sat. Her head nearly touched the top of the tunnel. She took a deep breath and smelled the wet earth inside the mountain. Then she felt a finger on her cheek near her lips. And next, warm lips on hers.

Electricity shot through her. She pressed her lips toward Ryan's and felt his tongue gently reach for hers. She thought about using her hands on his face or to pull him in closer, but there was something about kissing here in the pitch-black silence with only lips touching that overtook her. Shay knew she'd never forget this kiss. They sat for a moment, feeling the hot breath between them, until a noise behind them made them jump.

Garrett was close. Before they could reorganize, he plowed into them.

"What the hell? I thought I told you guys to crawl to the open part. You have fifty feet to go."

"It's really dark, Wayne. We can't see anything. We needed to take a break."

Garrett didn't respond. Shay heard a zipper, then Garrett digging around in his pack. Shay wondered if he was pulling out the duct tape to shut her up.

"Here. Strap this on." Garrett reached for Shay's hand and placed an object in it.

Shay thought of the blindfold game they used to play as kids. One kid wore a blindfold and the other kid tried to find objects that they couldn't guess. The object Shay held in her hand now felt like one of those lamps that miners wear to go gold digging. She felt around the lamp and flicked on the switch.

"Put it on your head," said Garrett.

"Thanks." Shay strapped it on and flicked a switch. Ryan shielded his eyes.

"Whoa!" And then, "Dude, do I get one?" asked Ryan.

"What do you think?"

Ryan turned around and moved into his tripod crawl as Shay lit the way. After a short distance, the tunnel opened up into the most incredible sight. The inside of the mountain looked like a huge cathedral. Golden rock formations plunged from the ceiling like gigantic icicles, while others that looked like waxy candles left too long to burn shot up from the ground. Pools gathered near rock families. Water trickled down icicle pillars into the ponds, causing them to glisten in the light of the headlamp.

"Wow," said Shay. "Amazing."

"Welcome to my studio," said Garrett.

"Super cool," said Shay overtaken by the atmosphere. "I've never seen anything like it." She meant it.

"Wait until you see it with the lights on," said Garrett in a proud voice.

Ryan refused to let him have his moment. "You've never been to the caverns?" said Ryan. "Not even on a field trip?"

"Nope," said Shay.

Garrett assumed the role of tour guide. "These are special caverns. I used to live here when I'd run away from Dad and had no place to go. I'd hitch a ride here with my twelve pack of chocolate pudding and live for a week. It's where I've had many of my inspirations."

"I can see why." Shay gazed down into the water and saw herself. She looked like a coal miner. She liked the way the water reflected the icicles and gave the illusion that they plunged far below the earth.

"See these?" said Garrett pointing at the formations hanging from above. "These are called stalactites. They're mineral deposits that drip down and make formations over time. The ones that grow from the ground are called stalagmites."

"Stalac-what?" asked Shay, mesmerized by their beauty.

"Stalagmites. Here's how you remember. The stalac*tites* need to hold on tight to the ceiling so they don't fall. Stalagmites are the opposite."

"Got it," said Shay.

"Now that we're done with our geology lesson, you think I might be able to get these ties cut off? They're cramping my style." Ryan held his bound hands over his head.

"Depends," said Garrett. "Are you good Ryan or bad Ryan?"

"Well, there's no place to run unless you think I might scale that stalag*tite* over there."

Garrett unzipped his bag. "Now, see, it's this smart-ass attitude of yours that gets you in trouble every time." Garrett pulled out a pair of scissors, waved them at Ryan as Shay grimaced, then cut the ties. Ryan shook his wrists in relief.

Shay looked at Ryan. Ryan had the same attitude with Garrett that he had with his Dad. She was afraid that, in this case, it might just get him killed.

"Hey, babe, watch the head lamp," said Ryan, shielding his eyes.

"Sorry." Shay turned her head back toward the cavern walls.

"Okay. Now if nobody else has any further requests, I can't wait to show Shay the Studio."

"Ahh, the big reveal," said Ryan.

They walked through paths in majestic caverns, climbing higher up and over huge rock formations that wound deep into the mountain. Shay heard water crashing. When they were near the water, Garrett stopped. He climbed up behind a stalactite and flipped a switch. The room lit with glowing lights. The sight was breathtaking. Huge stalactites plummeted from high above and filled the room. A blue lake to the side caught the waterfall Shay had heard earlier. Glistening waxy-looking ledges dipped in and out of shadows, hidden by the golden icicles.

"Help. Help." A faint voice could be heard behind the crashing water.

Shay scanned the sides of the wall. She caught a glimpse of black vertical bars. It reminded her of a tiger's cage she'd seen in movies with a traveling circus. The mist from the waterfall made it difficult to see. She squinted.

"Help, help," somebody cried again. Garrett ignored it and Ryan didn't seem to hear.

Shay thought it was coming from the cage. She scanned the side of the ledge and saw cages lining the left side. They were hidden in the shadows, but she could see stairs leading up.

"Welcome to the Studio," said Garrett, obviously proud of what he'd created here.

Shay and Ryan stared at him.

"Well? What do you think? Stunning, right?" Garrett threw down his pack. "I'm sorry. How rude of me. Let me show you to your room, Shay."

Shay looked at Ryan. He turned away.

Garrett laughed. "Oh, wait. You didn't tell her," he said pointing to Ryan.

"Tell me what?" said Shay.

Garrett paused, relishing in Shay's confusion. "Well, go on Ryan, tell her."

"*Tell me what?*" Shay yelled so loud it echoed off the walls.

Then a quiet voice, barely audible. "Shay. Is that you, Shay?"

Shay jerked her head up to the ledge. "Who's up there?" Then to Garrett, "Who is in that cage?"

"That's my next project, Ryan's sister."

Ryan turned back toward Shay. "I didn't have a choice."

Shay's mind swirled. "What choice? What are you talking about?"

Garrett was enjoying the unfolding scene. "Go on, Ryan. Tell your little girlfriend why you don't have a room in the Studio."

Ryan shook his head and turned away. "She's not my girlfriend. I just met her."

"Oh, for God's sake." He turned toward Shay and pointed at Ryan. "Cassanova here is my brother."

Shay stared at Garrett with wide eyes and a crinkled nose, her mouth hanging open. "Wait. What? How?"

"I love a good family reunion, don't you?" He laughed. Ryan scowled back at him.

"Knock it off, Wayne. You don't need to be an ass."

Garrett walked over to Ryan until his face was inches away. He glared for a minute then grabbed him by the throat and shoved him into the side of the cave. "Do I need to knock you out again? Give you a little of the Special K then spend some time with your girlfriend? Did you forget who you're talking to?"

Ryan choked and struggled, but he was no match for Garrett. "Let him go," screamed Shay.

Garrett dropped Ryan, who slumped to the ground and gasped for air. "Aw, isn't that sweet, even after he lured you here for my art work. So loyal."

"I didn't have a choice, Shay." Ryan looked like he was about to cry.

Shay couldn't decide if she was more disgusted, angry, or afraid. Betrayal was a thread that wove through her life. Each time she'd trusted someone, they made her wish she hadn't. Now it looked like it was going to cost her life. Worse than that, she was going to have to watch Ronda lose hers. She didn't want to talk anymore. She didn't want to hear Ryan tell his lies or Garrett play his mind games. She just wanted to go up to her room and get away from these two crazies.

"Can I go to my room now?" asked Shay.

Garrett walked over and touched Shay's arm. "Don't you think we should spend a little time together first?"

"Don't you touch her," yelled Ryan.

Garrett shifted his attention to Ryan, who was still lying on the ground holding his throat. "Oh, for God's sake, you *are* stupid. How is it that we share the same mother?" He kicked Ryan in the side. Ryan groaned and rolled into the fetal position. "Freakin' wuss."

"I'm really tired, Wayne," said Shay. "I really do like the Studio. It's beautiful."

Garrett looked around the room and smirked. "It is, isn't it? Thanks for noticing. You'd probably be a good artist, too."

Shay forced a smile. Garrett pointed in the direction of the stairs. "Right this way, Shay."

As they walked up the stairs, Garrett said, "You know, Shay, you were always one of my favorites. I like you. But I can't trust you anymore after our swim. And you've seen things. It would hurt my ability to do my work if people found out."

"I won't tell anybody. I swear," said Shay.

"But you already have—and in such short time, too. You told Ryan and you barely even know him." He laughed. "Obviously."

As they reached the top of the staircase, Shay saw the row of cages. All were empty but one. Ronda lay on a mat on the ground, barely able to speak. "What's wrong with her? What did you do to her?"

"Nothing I won't do to you, too. Don't worry." He pointed to the cage next to Ronda. "Here's your room. Compliments of Barnum and Bailey's."

Shay wasn't sure what that meant.

Garrett read her confusion, "What? Never been to the circus?"

Shay shook her head. "I don't believe in the circus."

"Oh, whatever. Who doesn't believe in the circus? Anyway, now's your chance to get an up-close view."

He pushed Shay into the cage and locked the door. The cage was too short to stand upright. There was a towel thrown down on the floor. A coffee can sat in one corner. A bottle of water and a granola bar were in the another. Shay scrunched down and went in. "Looks like you've thought of everything."

"Yep," said Garrett. "Lights out in five. I'm beat." He turned to walk away then turned back and yelled, "My work is not as easy as it seems. Tomorrow, I'll bring you a friend."

The ground was cold, and Shay wondered how she'd ever sleep. She scooted up against the back of the cage, looking out at the cavern under the glow of the lights. The bars on her back were cold. She heard Ronda whimper.

"Oh, honey, are you okay?" Before the words left Shay's mouth, she was pretty sure Ronda would never be okay.

Ronda could barely speak. "It's so good to see you, but I'm so sad you're here." She paused. "This guy's insane."

"We'll figure this out. It's going to be okay," said Shay.

Ronda nodded and then the room went dark.

Shay and Ronda fell asleep to the sound of the waterfall crashing against the pool below.

Chapter 12

con·ster
kan stər
Noun
An app for tracking criminals in the beta stage

When Shay woke up, Ronda was huddled in the back corner of her cage puking. The putrid smell soaked into everything. The sound of the vomit splashing into more vomit told Shay Ronda's bucket was almost full. No telling what else was mixed in there. She hoped it didn't overflow all over the cage.

Shay sat up and scooted next to her friend. Ronda looked up from her now dry heaving. Shay reached through the bars and rubbed her limp shoulder.

Ronda wiped her mouth and started to cry. "This dude's insane."

"Start from the beginning," Shay whispered. "Tell me what happened."

Ronda leaned away from Shay and put her bucket in the far corner. "Smells awful. Sorry." She laid her head against the cage bars and closed her eyes, tears still streaming down her dirt-stained cheeks. "I'm so dizzy. Must be the drugs."

Shay listened and waited. "Take your time. I'm here all night."

Ronda smiled weakly at Shay's attempt to lighten the scene. "He took me, Shay. I was sleeping, and he just came in and grabbed me out of my bed."

Shay rubbed her eyes. Her head pounded. She felt like she'd dragged Ronda into this. "I'm so sorry, Ronda. I should have never come to the house that—"

Ronda stopped her. "This is not your fault, Shay. This is my stupid-ass brother's fault. They're like some freaky killer duo or something."

Shay stared at Ronda. "What?"

"They're like—I don't know ... working as a team or something." Ronda shrugged her shoulders and curled her lip in disgust.

Shay couldn't believe that Ryan was in on it. He felt different to her, like someone she could really like. How did she miss that he was involved with a killer? She thought back to the Shed and his over-involved role in Julia's life. She wondered how far it went back. Had he set Julia up from the beginning or did something happen later that turned him? Shay couldn't wrap her mind around it. Clearly, he'd led her into this trap as well. Her jaw clenched, and she felt her shoulders tighten. She hit the rock with the back of her fist.

"How could he do this? Do you think he was forced like he says?" Shay really hoped he was.

"More like he's a pathological liar. He's always been jealous of me," said Ronda.

Shay's head swirled as she tried to process the Ryan Ronda described. "Why jealous?"

"Because he's adopted. My parents couldn't have any kids, so they got him. Then I came along," said Ronda. "The surprise bio-baby. He's always considered himself the consolation prize."

"I had no idea," said Shay. "Guess it's good to be an only child sometimes. Do you know anything about his parents?"

Ronda shook her head. "Not much. Just that he was found alone with an older brother. A neighbor heard them crying and called the cops. They were locked inside a room filled with feces and garbage."

"That's horrible. What happened to the brother?"

"My parents don't really talk a lot about it. Mom just says she fell in love with Ryan and took him home. She says that's where he belonged."

"And then you came along." Shay smiled.

"Yep. I don't think I can ever forgive him for what he let Garrett do to me." Ronda turned away and looked down, pulling her arms tighter around her knees. She started to cry again. "Nobody wants their first to go down like that."

Shay stared at Ronda. She leaned closer to her face and smelled the vomit on her breath. "Wait. You're a virgin?"

"Not now," said Ronda. "In fact, I never want to have sex again. It was horrible."

Shay paused and chose her words carefully. "But you said you had sex with that Junior over Christmas break. You said that Levi and I should try it because it was so great."

Ronda lay back against the bars of the cage. She wiped her tears and looked down at the ground. She traced a heart in the red dirt bottom with her finger.

"I know. I lied."

"Why, though?" asked Shay, watching her closely.

"Because you were always telling me things about you and Levi, and your creepy graveyard fetish. I felt like I needed to keep up."

Shay sat back against the cage and scooted as close as she could get to her friend. Ronda always tried to come off so cool and confident, like nothing and nobody bothered her. She was tall and had the type of presence every teen wants but not many can master. When she walked into a room, people turned and stared in recognition of her alpha presence. They might not have liked her, but they wouldn't dare let her know that. She could be a mean girl when she wanted to be.

Most of the time, Ronda acted like the world was there to serve her. Everyone at school thought she was a spoiled princess bitch. The one percent of Jefferson, with her two-parent professional family, nice house, sexy brother, and sweet puppy. The dancer, cheerleader, college-bound privilege who would rather step on a classmate than over one.

But Shay knew the truth: Ronda was like any other teen in Jefferson. She just wanted to fit in. She struggled with family, with peers, with being the type of friend she wanted to have. She worried about what group to hang out with at lunch to secure her status in the pack that is teendom. She felt anxious about going to high school and having to redefine her role and position in the social hierarchy. She wanted to be loved, appreciated, and recognized. She wanted people to listen.

Shay reached through the bars and held out her hand. Ronda looked up and grabbed it. "I'm sorry I lied to you," she said. "I just wanted you to be my best friend."

They sat holding hands, listening to the sound of the waterfall crashing. Their friendship had shifted and they both felt it. The connection that so often lived just below the surface had rooted down deeper. They both felt grateful.

"I'm so sorry, Ronda."

"For what?"

"For all of it. For not being more sensitive to your feelings when I talked about Levi. For this. For Garrett. For Ryan. For all of it."

"It's not your fault."

"I don't know about fault, but I just feel sad inside that you've had to go through this and I want you to know that."

"I do."

"Annnd ..."

"And what?"

"I want you to know I love you and I am going to get you out of this. I promise."

Ronda smiled and nodded. "I love you, too. Uh-oh." She leaned over and grabbed the bucket again. "I just feel so nauseous. Did I tell you what I think happened?"

"You mean, like how you were really faded last night."

"Yeah. At our house, he shot me up with something that paralyzed me. I was completely aware of what was happening but couldn't move anything."

"How horrible!" said Shay, feeling her words were insufficient.

"He dragged me here and—" Ronda's voice gave out.

"It's okay, it's okay, Mi-o. We don't have to talk about it if you don't want to."

Ronda nodded and attempted a slight smile at Shay's attempt at creating a Hawaiian nickname. Blood strung through her hair where she said Garrett had hit her with a rock for no apparent reason. Her eyes were red and swollen. Mascara stained her face. Her yellow shirt had turned brown from the red dirt and ripped so that it wouldn't stay on her shoulder. She looked broken.

"I didn't want to, Shay. He made me … and with some girl's dead body in the room."

Shay wondered if Ronda was in shock. She'd seen that on TV when characters would keep revisiting conversations they'd just had, like when she fell off her bar and got a concussion. She knew she had to get Ronda out of there.

"Gross. Freakin' creeper. That must have been horrible."

"Thinks he's an artist. He's demented," said Ronda.

Shay nodded. "Yeah. We saw him staging his last project." Shay paused. "Some older lady. She's up at the geocache by the swing."

"So that's where he took her. I was just so relieved to have them both gone. How'd he get you?"

Shay looked out into the caverned room. The crashing water covered the sound as she sat whispering with Ronda. She wasn't sure where Garrett was. It kept her on edge. "Well, I have your brother to thank for that."

"Please don't call him that. We shouldn't call him that. He's not my brother."

"I know you hate him right now. So do I. But I have a hard time thinking he'd do this on his own."

"Really? What's wrong with you? He definitely did it."

Shay paused, questioning her own sanity. "I can't tell you what it is. I feel like there's more to the story. What really matters is that you're my friend and I'm going to make a plan. We're going to get you out of here if I have to dig through this damn cave with my fingernails," said Shay, pawing at the air.

Ronda smiled. "I suppose it's my own fault for trying to set you up in the first place. I'd love to hear your plan on this great escape because pretty sure I'm the next art project."

Shay whispered, "Don't worry. I'm working on it." She pointed to her head and tapped her temple.

A clatter below made Ronda and Shay lunge to the front of their cages. Garrett stood looking up at them, banging a pan with a rock. It clanged and echoed off the sides of the cavern. Ryan was passed out in the same place they'd seen him last night. He looked dead.

"Good morning, ladies. Catching up?" he asked. "Hungry? We've got a big day ahead."

Ronda scuffled back to the back of the cage where Garrett couldn't see her. Shay yelled down, "Not hungry, but Ronda's sick. She needs to dump her bucket."

Garrett ignored her. He walked over to Ryan and kicked him. "Wake up, little brother. You're in charge."

Ryan rolled over and moaned. He looked up at Garrett. "What time is it?"

"It's time for our big day. It's Saturday. We have so much to do. I just love weekends, don't you?"

Saturdays *were* a big day for Garrett. Shay remembered from the police report that he liked to stage his kills on Saturday, then celebrate by trolling the bars on Hillcrest for victims for another. He was definitely escalating and had moved beyond just Saturdays, as evidenced by the display the night before.

Ryan rolled over and got to his feet. He dusted off his pants. "Where's the next cache site?" he asked.

"It's like you read my mind, bro," Garrett said. "That's exactly what I'm going to explore before the hordes of lake-people come out. I need somewhere special for that sister of yours. Somewhere where she'll be seen, but we won't be seen at work. I like to do my art in private."

Ryan walked over to the supply stash, popped open a bottle of water and unwrapped a cereal bar. "What about the spot over by the bridge. Jace's Point, I think they call it."

Garrett smiled. "See, now that's how I know we're related. We've got a feel for the land."

Shay watched as Garrett prepared a small bag for his scouting trip. He threw in a few bars, water, knife, and a rope. Ryan was acting oddly. Last night Garrett kicked the shit out of him and today, they were running this bro-mance. Garrett turned to leave.

"Wait," said Ryan. "You need to leave the key."

Garrett squinted. "And why do I need to do that?"

The next part of the conversation was too quiet for Shay to hear. Ryan walked right up next to Garrett, pointed up to the cages, and laughed. Garrett laughed back and reached in his pocket and pulled out the key. "That's my bro!" he said, and left the cave.

As soon as Garret left, Ryan began to pace. He walked out of the cathedral room toward the exit and disappeared for a bit.

Shay turned toward Ronda. "Now's our chance. Do you feel healthy enough to get out of this place?"

"I can barely move. But, yeah. It's either that or die a horribly gruesome death, right?" said Ronda.

Shay felt around the bars of the cage. She had no idea how to pick a lock. She scanned the cage, looking for a sharp implement to stick in the keyhole.

"Do you see anything that might help us?" she asked.

Ronda rolled over on her hands and knees and scoured the floor. Shay did the same. All they found was red dirt.

Below, Ryan ran back into the cathedral room. He rushed over behind a rock and pulled out an iPad. He turned it on. Pad in hand, he ran up the stairs to the cages.

He reached the cages and plopped down between Shay and Ronda. "Listen. We have to act fast. I'm going to help you get out of here, but we have to be quick about it."

Shay stared at Ryan. "How do we know you're not setting us up?"

"You don't," said Ryan. "But your choices are pretty limited. I'll explain everything. But we've got to move *now*."

Last time Shay trusted Ryan, she ended up here, locked in this cage. Her feelings for him had blinded her to his true agenda. The same thing had happened with Levi. She needed a moment.

Shay put up her hand. "Don't rush me, Ryan. I need to think," she said. She looked at Ronda. "Okay?"

Ronda nodded, then glared at Ryan.

Shay closed her eyes. She listened to the sound of the water. She pictured herself in the flow of that water, moving easily. Her heart was telling her to trust Ryan even though it made no sense. She questioned it, though, because last time it was wrong, and she ended up here. It started beating fast, letting her know they did need to hurry. Her technology break had been good for her inner listening. She couldn't remember the last time she'd gone so many hours without a phone. She felt like she could hear her heart better. She hadn't had a freak-out the whole time in the cave. She could hear that voice inside, her strongest guide. She opened her eyes. It told her to give Ryan another chance.

"I'm listening," she said.

Ryan sat up and pointed to the iPad. "I'll get you guys out and we'll head up to the bridge where we can get service. We'll make sure we don't cross paths by tracking him on Conster."

"Conster?" Shay asked.

"It's a new app to track criminals. It's in the beta phase at one of those secret Silicon Valley labs. It's like Find Friends only it works on a chip. When a criminal drops into the system, they chip them so they can track them. They inject the chip into his bloodstream while he's knocked out. Half the time they don't even know. If criminals make a big deal about it, other people just think they're being crazy."

"What? Never heard of it," said Ronda.

"Well, I overheard the chief and your dad talking about how they'd heard rumblings of it up at the courthouse and how they thought it was the greatest, so I had one of my techy friends look into it, and, *voila*, meet Conster."

Ronda hadn't said a word. She was staring at Ryan like he was the person she hated most in the world. "Are we going before the *artist* gets back or are we going to Yelp new apps?"

"Sis, I know you're mad at me, but I had no choice. I'm really sorry. I'll make it up to you," he said. "Trust me. The story goes deeper than you think."

He pulled out the key to open the cages. First he unlocked Shay's. She crawled out and stood up, dusting the red dirt off. Then he unlocked Ronda's. Ronda grabbed her bucket of vomit and heaved it at him. The vomit splashed all over Ryan. The sour milk smell made Shay gag. She put her hand over her mouth and gasped.

Ryan stood up and wiped chunks of vomit off his eyelids. He stared at Ronda. "I deserved that," he said.

"Yes," said Ronda, "you did."

Ronda crawled out of the cage. They rushed down the stairs and into the large cathedral room. Ryan grabbed the supply bag. "Stay close and follow me."

They scuttled back out the way they came. Over the rocks, down the paths, past the stalactites and stalagmites, past the lakes and to the big boulder. They each lined up against the big boulder and pushed it out of the way.

Shay took a deep breath. The sun was just coming up. She had never felt as free as she did at this moment, such a feeling of possibility. She felt strong. Empowered. Like Scout. Finally, like Scout. She thought it strange that it took nearly dying to feel so alive. This was the part of her she wanted to keep alive. The part that was the child inside her that realized she had a clear purpose: to help her friend escape the cave alive.

Ryan fired up the iPad. "Let me pull this up so we can see how close he is. I'd like to take the lake route to the bridge, so I can wash the vomit off." He gave Ronda a look.

"Don't even start with me," she said.

He laughed. "I know, I know."

Ryan pulled up Garrett on the tracker. "This is good. He's over on the other side. That chip he got at Crystal Creek is paying off." He had taken the low road in the opposite direction.

They moved over the rocks toward the water. "Why don't ex-cons know about this app? Makes no sense. If you can find out, they can certainly find out," said Ronda.

"That's true. I don't know. All I know is my friend found it in a dark hole and pulled it up. We found him on there."

As they reached the water, Ryan handed the iPad to Shay. "Hold this." He stepped in and grimaced. The water was freezing. He kneeled down and tried to wash the vomit off his face.

Shay watched Garrett move on the iPad. He definitely looked like he was moving away from them, but Shay's stomach was wrenching. She had a very strong sense he was close by.

"Let's go, Ryan," said Ronda. "We need to get up to the road." Ronda must have sensed it, too.

The rocks were slippery down near the water. Ronda struggled. Ryan and Shay held her up on each side. The three walked like that under the bridge and up the hill to the other side.

Ryan pointed to a hole in the fence at the top. "We just need to get there. Then we'll walk up the road and flag a car. Should just take us five minutes."

"You okay?" Shay asked Ronda.

"Do you need me to carry you?" Ryan asked.

"I'm fine," she said to Shay, then looked at Ryan." And no."

They made their way to the hill. As they climbed up, their feet slipped in the loose gravel. The incline was too steep for them.

"Let's head just a little further down to that grove of trees. The hill's easier there and we can come back up the path.

The three headed toward the trees. Ronda's limp got harder to manage the further they went. They passed through the grove then turned back up to a path that led to the road. Shay heard a car whiz by. They were so close.

Ryan turned to wait for Ronda and said. "When we get up there, you two wait on the side of the road. I'll hold back. Somebody's more apt to pick up the two of you. When they stop, I'll come out."

"Lame," said Shay. "But you're probably right." Shay couldn't trust Ryan completely. She felt they had to work with him to get away from Garrett, but she was also fully aware that he could be tricking them again.

"Not to mention you're covered in putrid vomit smell," said Ronda. "They'd pull over, smell you, and take off."

"Yep. Just don't leave me out here," said Ryan. "My death won't be pretty after helping you both get away. Wayne had big plans for you."

They walked the final steps up to the road and heard something wrestle in the bushes that startled them. They jumped.

"Going somewhere?" asked Garrett, pointing a gun.

Chapter 13

re·fresh
ree frəsh
verb
to make new

Ryan looked down at his pad. "Wait. How?"

Garrett laughed. "Bro, did you forget to refresh? Guess we know who snagged the brains in this gene pool."

Frustrated, Ryan threw the iPad down and stomped on it.

Garrett's face turned to steel. "Oh, that's going to cost you little brother."

Ryan's eyes widened as he watched Garrett come toward him, hands out ready to grab his throat. Ryan grabbed a rock to protect himself, but instead got a kick to the face. Garrett's boot hit Ryan's flesh and made Shay cry out. Ryan fell back onto the gravel. His head slammed against the rocks. Blood streamed from his nose. Garrett kicked him again in the ribs, hard. He stood over him and stomped a boot down on Ryan's chest.

"You broke my fucking nose," said Ryan trying to push his nose back so it felt normal.

"And you broke my fucking iPad." Garrett picked up his boot and stomped it again hard on Ryan's chest. Ryan gasped for air and seemed unable to breathe in. His eyes opened wide and he grabbed his throat. "Now we're even."

Ryan gasped. "Even? I can't breathe!"

"Bonus rib to go with that broken nose. Welcome to my world."

After the air finally sunk into his lungs, Ryan writhed in pain on the ground. Shay and Ronda watched, unsure what to do next.

Garrett turned. "And then we have you two. Out for a stroll?" He walked toward Ronda as she cowered behind Shay. "Did you forget we're going to spend some special time together again today?"

Shay stepped in front of her friend. "Why does she get all the fun?" she said, reaching up and touching Garrett's arm. "Why not me?"

Garrett tilted his head and stared at Shay. He didn't speak. He looked down at her hand on his arm and backed away. Shay held his gaze. His icy blue eyes softened, looked confused. As quickly as he had softened, he hardened and grabbed Shay's hair. "I know what you're trying to do and it's not going to work. We already went for a swim, remember Shay?

Good try."

He grabbed Ronda by the hair with his other hand. He used their hair like reins and steered them toward the street. "I've got special plans for you two. You're going to be my best works yet."

In the next moment, Shay felt her hair release and heard a loud crack. Somehow Ryan had rallied and hit Garrett with a rock on the back of his head, knocking him to the ground.

"Run!" he yelled.

Shay grabbed Ronda's hand and hurried as fast as she could toward the highway.

Garrett screamed like a wounded animal. The guttural sound made Shay think he transformed into something not human. It started low, like a roar, and ended in the sound of a deranged, out of control animal ready to kill. "You're a dead man!"

Grunts and the smacking of fists made Shay turn and look back. It was like watching Garrett punch, and kick, and roll around on the ground with Daddy Dean all over again. Shay was a child standing on the black welded fence, watching and taking bets on who would win. Garrett would kill Ryan. He was bigger than Ryan and his anger made him more dangerous. Shay wondered if he would ever be able to forget, or if he would just keep punishing people in search of some twisted revenge.

Ronda broke her from her fight trance. "Hurry, Shay. I hear something."

The sound of a car in the distance brought Shay back to the moment. The highway was close. "Run!"

"I can barely walk," said Ronda.

"I know the feeling," said Shay.

She put Ronda's arm over her shoulder and started to run. "Hold on." They moved together like a lame sack-racing team.

As the car came closer, sirens sounded. The wails pierced the lake's peaceful quiet, blaring until the car came to a screeching halt along the roadside. Tires spewed gravel in every direction. Through the trees, Shay could see at least four cars with red strobe lights flashing. Shay looked back and saw Garrett running into the forest. Ryan lay in a bloody heap in the gravel. Garrett looked back and his eyes met hers for a quick flash. For the first time since she had been small and seen him fighting with Daddy Dan, he looked terrified.

A team of officers piled out of the cars, weapons drawn. Ronda and Ryan heard Chief Reynolds say, "Get the dogs! He's here close. It's firing on the tracker."

A large German Shepherd jumped out of the car. "Come on, Cain. Go find the bad guy," said his handler.

Nose to ground, Cain sniffed straight for the trees. Ronda jumped to her feet and ran down the hill.

"Dad!"

Cain ran over to her. "Good boy, Cain. Go get him. He's in there," Ronda yelled. "Get the bad guy!" Cain dashed into the trees.

Chief Reynolds ran to Ronda. His huge oversized frame wrapped around her like a warm blanket. He held her tight and his body shook like he was crying. After a moment, held her out in front of him.

"Are you okay?" he asked. He reached behind and grabbed Shay's arm to bring her closer. Before Ronda could answer, he wrapped them both in his big bear hug cocoon. Shay felt safe for the first time in as long as she could remember.

"Yes. We're okay. Ryan's up on the hill," said Ronda, pointing back. "He's a mess."

Her father let go and picked up the radio. "Code 11-41, Code 11-41."

He listened. From the other end, "I have your location at I-5 just north of Sandy Creek. Sending ambo."

"Roger that. Thanks, Fred. And hurry. It's Ryan."

"Copy that, Chief."

The chief set the radio down and surveyed the scene. "Take me to him."

Shay and Ronda walked toward Ryan just as two officers yelled down, "We need medical up here."

The chief ran toward Ryan, leaving Shay and Ronda behind. Shay grabbed Ronda's arm and swung it over her shoulder as she grabbed her waist. She knew Ronda was looking for the right time to tell her father that Ryan had been on it from the start.

"First things first," Shay whispered. "We don't even know if he's going to make it."

Ronda nodded. "It's going to kill my dad."

Shay side-hugged her. "I know."

Shay and Ronda reached Ryan. An officer was bent down checking his pulse. "He's still breathing, but barely. He's pretty messed up."

Ryan was out cold. His handsome face was cut and dripping red. His lip was split. Drool dripped out the side of his gaping mouth. His tooth was knocked out and lying on the ground. His eyes were swollen shut. Shay wondered how someone could do so much damage in such a short time.

She had so many mixed emotions. Ryan had helped her from the beginning when she crawled to the shed. He was warm and kind. She connected with him. She like-liked him even. She'd kissed him. And yet, he had helped Garrett kill people. She wasn't sure how deep it went. He clearly was a follower when it came to Garrett, and she could see how powerless he was when it came to him. She wondered if he even had a choice. She also knew everyone always has a choice.

Then there was the part about how he'd saved them from dying a sadistic death at the hands of Garrett. He threw himself in the fire so they could make a break for it. He finally figured out how to stand up to Garrett, so he could protect them.

In the distance, Shay heard Cain bark twice. The chief looked into the forest. "That's Cain's signal. I think they caught the bastard."

A few minutes later, Garrett appeared. His hands were cuffed behind his back. His brown sweaty curls hung across his dirty, blood-covered face. A big rip across the flesh of his thigh showed Cain's work.

"Your damn dog bit me," he said as he walked by Chief Reynolds.

"That's the least of your worries."

Garrett glared at the older man, and then shifted his anger toward Shay. "I'm not done with you." Shay turned away.

"Get him out of here," said the chief, dismissing Garrett and his threats. He reached out a hand and rubbed Shay's shoulder. "Don't worry about him, Shay. Where he's going, you'll never have to think about him again."

Shay wondered if that was possible. She'd thought about him for as long as she could remember. To her, he represented the real-life version of what could go wrong in someone who didn't feel heard and loved. It didn't matter that his parents chose him. He wasn't an oops baby to them. They'd rescued him from a horrible situation and gave him a family and a home. Still, he never felt wanted. Shay wasn't sure he ever would.

The siren from the ambulance arriving and the siren taking Garrett away danced together in the still morning air stirring up the silence. Paramedics ran up the hill and tended to Ryan. The chief reminded them they were working on his son. He told them he'd meet them at Mercy Hospital in an hour.

"Let's get you two cleaned up and down to the station. We need to get the whole story so that bastard gets the needle."

Chapter 14

Viral
vahy-*ruh* l
adjective
becoming very popular by circulating quickly from
person to person, especially through the Internet:
the most memorable viral videos;
This book is already viral two weeks before its official publication date.

The chief drove the black sedan down I-5 toward central Redding. He'd called ahead to tell Shay's parents and Ronda's mom to meet them there. Ronda and Shay had piled in the back together. Even a car seat's distance seemed too much after what they'd been through together. The drive to the station gave time to answer unanswered questions. Shay let Ronda go first.

"How did you find us?' she asked.

"Two things," her dad said, looking at them in the rearview mirror. "First, the video clip you uploaded on YouTube went viral. Turns out people have weird obsessions about serial killers."

"Shay's brainchild," said Ronda proudly. "She figured if we could catch him in the act you'd have the proof you needed to put him away forever." Ronda smiled at Shay.

"I'm just glad it went through. I was uploading it when I was knocked out."

"Wait. Had you just finished recording Garrett?"

Shay realized what she had just done, but she wasn't sure how to back out of it. "Um ... yes?"

"Someone else was there." It was a statement, not a question.

"Yes." Shay answered, more firmly this time. Ronda and Shay shared a look.

"You knew him?"

The air in the car stunk. It smelled like smoke had been poorly covered up with pine air freshener. The silence hung in the stale smell until Ronda couldn't stand it anymore.

"Dad, it was Ryan," said Ronda.

Chief Reynolds pulled the car off to the side of the road, and stared for a solid minute shifting his eyes from one girl to the other. "Ryan? Are you sure?"

Ronda spilled the story. "Dad, yes. I'm sure. I don't know when it started, but Ryan dated Julia and then she ended up dead. Garrett says Ryan's his brother. I don't know how he knows that. He totally set me up. I hate him."

The chief stared straight ahead. Shay watched his jaw tighten and his eyes squint as he pulled back onto the road drove in stoic silence. It was clear they needed to give him a minute to process.

They drove past the boat shops and burger bars that lined the sides of the interstate. They passed pickups with fancy speedboats hooked to their hitches on their way to the lake. The snow had half-melted off Shasta. Lassen was barely capped at the very top. The Baldy Mountains on the opposite side of the Valley were bare. Soon, temperatures in the hundreds would be punishing lawns and locals. This certainly wasn't the launch Shay had imagined for her last summer before high school.

Ronda couldn't stand it anymore. "Dad? Could that be true? Could Garrett be Ryan's brother?"

The chief stared back in the rearview. He paused, then quietly said, "Yes."

"How?" asked Ronda.

"It goes back to a case we had on the rez." He hesitated as if he thought he'd already said too much. "Garrett was already spoken for, but the couple couldn't take both of them, and we thought it best to make a clean break. The family who adopted Garrett moved away, but I guess they came back."

Shay looked at Ronda who had her face squished up in a confused look. "You said there were two ways you found us?" Ronda asked.

The chief took a breath. He seemed relieved to leave the topic of Ryan's origins. "Yes," he said. "The first YouTube. The second was Conster. Our IT guy tracked him using this new technology—"

"We know about it," said Ronda. "So do they."

He ignored her comment. "It's in beta test, and it definitely has some tweaks that need to be ironed out. We think it'll help us catch the bad guys. If we can just get it past these State of Jefferson people who think we're always on the take to invade their rights."

Shay spoke up. "The video and Conster helped you find us?"

He nodded. "Probably our greatest lead of all was Garrett himself."

"How?" asked Shay.

"Turns out he really likes people to see his work," said the chief.

"You mean like his geocache displays?" asked Shay.

"Well, there's that. But we think that came later. We're still piecing the puzzle together."

Ronda leaned forward. "What do you mean later?"

"We're obviously still investigating, but we have a hunch he's connected with a number of runaways that have gone missing across the state in the past month."

"How many?" asked Shay.

"Four that we know of. One was floating down Clear Creek between county lines and the sheriffs were standing on each side blowing the body into the other guy's jurisdiction."

Ronda and Shay looked at each other puzzled. "Why would they do that?" Ronda asked.

"Politics of crime. Nobody wants more crime stats in their county than they have to have. Looks bad on graphs. Brings down property values."

Ronda rolled her eyes. "What about the victim's property rights?"

The chief said, "I know, honey. You're totally right."

Shay wanted to get back to how Garrett gave himself away. "How did he tip you off? Garrett, I mean," she said.

"This guy loves to display his work. He needs an audience. If nobody sees what he's done, he gets antsy."

"He thinks he's an artist," said Shay under her breath.

"More like a sadist," said Ronda.

"What he ended up doing was calling the anonymous tip line to report a body posed at the dump. That week was a slow trash week, and nobody saw his clever display of a runaway spread-eagle over old tires."

"How'd you know it was him? The call was anonymous, right?" asked Shay.

"Well, there was one more thing. Garrett was down at Sports and Snacks bragging to Buzzy about how he was an artist and had his gallery spread around town. People just had to notice his genius. He slammed his piece on the counter and said he was going to be famous. Buzzy called me after he left."

"His gallery?" asked Ronda. "How many?"

"Five that we know about. Still under investigation for now. He was fast and furious. We think he must have started the same day he left Crystal Creek."

"Five," said Ronda, leaning forward and grabbing the back of his head rest.

"Five that we know about," said Chief Reynolds.

Ronda sat back against the back of the dark gray seat. She leaned over and laid her head on Shay's shoulder, then down on her lap. Shay stroked her hair, so thankful they weren't numbers six and seven.

"We're just so grateful you found us," said Shay. "Thank you, Chief."

"Me, too," he said. Shay thought she saw a tear bead up in his left eye. "You were very brave to do what you did to help us catch this bastard."

The chief hung a right down Highway 44 and passed over the Sacramento River. The sky was cobalt blue with china-white cumulus clouds that hung over the red clay bluffs. The scene looked like a child's painting before life turned to shit. Shay wondered if that was a real place, that fairy tale land of chimney smoke and pink-curtained windows she'd seen kids draw. She wondered if she and Ronda could get anywhere close to that place after having seen what they'd seen. She desperately wanted to. She was almost positive Garrett couldn't and that was just fine with her.

They drove into downtown to the main RPD station. Downtown was filled with historical red brick buildings, tattoo parlors, breweries, and homeless people with shaggy dogs. The fire department and city hall were nestled up against the foster care licensing center, Manny's Tacos, and an alley known for the needles left behind. Locals really only went downtown these days if they had to go to the courthouse. That was where Shay's mom worked. It sat right next to the police station.

When they walked into the station, Shay's mom ran to her and started to cry. "Oh, honey. I was so worried. I was at work getting some overflow done and I heard the call come through dispatch. I just had a hunch and looked up the warrant. It was for Garrett and I just knew."

"I'm all right, Mom. Don't worry," said Shay. She was relieved Alex wasn't there.

"Did he hurt you, honey?"

"Not me." Shay looked at Ronda.

Shay's mom turned toward Ronda. "Oh, I'm so sorry, Ro."

Ronda started to cry. "It's okay, Momma Burke." Mrs. Burke's arms wrapped her in a hug.

Chief Reynolds said, "It's been a tough day." He reached out and touched Ronda's shoulder. "Mom should be here any minute Ronda. She was in the middle of an emergency surgery and couldn't leave the hospital." He gave Shay's mom a look Shay had a hard time translating. He almost seemed embarrassed that her mom needed to hug his daughter.

Ronda sobbed harder. She caught her dad's look, too. She hated needing her mom, because she just couldn't be sure she'd be there. Shay was happy to lend Ronda her mom, even if it wasn't the same.

The police station was a bustling place with phones ringing and people coming and going. Bustling was the last thing Shay needed. When the chief suggested she and Ronda clean up in the bathroom, she was relieved. They made their way past stacks of paper to a door in the back.

Shay liked being removed from the chaos of crime. Ronda leaned over the sink and washed the blood off her face. "Is it over yet?" she said, staring down at the reddish-brown swirl as it drained.

"God, I hope so," said Shay. "Are you okay? You've been through a lot." Shay attempted to wash her arms off before putting on one of the RPD T-shirts the officer had given them to wear.

"I don't even know. I feel like I'm dreaming." Ronda turned off the water and looked in the mirror. "I need to shower for like three days solid."

"The water police will come get you in this drought," said Shay. California was in the worst drought of its history. Everybody was on notice to cut back.

"Let them come." Ronda put on her shirt. "All I want to do is go home, hide in the bathroom where it's safe, and never come out."

Shay knew how she felt. She wasn't sure where to go from here. She couldn't get excited about graduation or summer or anything. Still, she felt like she needed to cheer Ronda up. "The good news is we caught the bad guy. No more dead bodies on display."

Ronda nodded and leaned up against the wall. "You're right. I do feel really good about that. I'm just so tired."

"Me, too." Shay walked over and hugged Ronda. She was limp and barely hugged back. "Let's go see if your mom is here."

When they walked out of the bathroom, Ronda's mom rushed over and hugged her. Ronda again made little effort to hug back.

Shay's mom grabbed Shay's hand and smiled. "Oh, that's better. But let's get you home and really cleaned up. We can come back later when you're feeling better and answer some questions. They said that was okay."

Shay was relieved. The last thing she wanted to do was relive the past twenty-four hours. She turned toward Ronda. "You going to be okay?"

Ronda's mom side-hugged her and said, "She's going to be fine, aren't you, honey?"

Shay thought she saw Ronda pull away just a little. "Right behind you."

"Call you later," said Shay. They both knew that'd be a text and not for a few days.

As Shay and her mom left the station, Shay felt her stomach growl. She realized the last solid food she'd eaten was the peanut butter cracker at Ronda's house. "Can we stop somewhere? I'm starving."

"Of course, honey. What are you hungry for?"

"How about that Déjà Blu place across from the old mall? Or we could go to Jaque's for a huge porterhouse."

Both places were Reading hot spots. Déjà Blu had a bakery that smelled up the city with fresh cinnamon buns. They also had the best shrimp salad in town. Jaque's was a 1960s holdover famous for their unwillingness to make any PC accommodations to customers. They served up the best steaks in town, with salad slathered in blue cheese dressing. There was no holding the dressing. It was dark inside day and night. There were only a few tables and a long bar. There were no reservations. At night, the wait could be two hours long. The bartender was known for his strong drinks and tall tales, but since Shay was too young to sit at the bar she couldn't confirm, although she'd heard her parents talk about it many times.

"Let's try Déjà Blu today," said her mom. "I could really use a piece of Dottie's rhubarb pie."

"Sounds perfect."

The restaurant was a quick five blocks from the station. They parked on California Street in front and walked inside. The smell made Shay's stomach growl. A young hostess in a white cotton dress and brunette hair wrapped up in a high bun greeted them.

"How many?"

"Just two," said Shay's mom.

"Great. This okay?" She pointed to a deep red vinyl covered circular booth in the far corner. It was blocked with a high partition and very private.

"Perfect," they said at the same time.

They settled in and looked at the menus. An older woman in a white dress and blue apron came over to take their drink order. Her name tag said "Hello, I'm Bonnie." Bonnie looked more like a nurse then a server. Shay ordered an iced tea.

"We'll both have the shrimp salad," said Shay's mom. "Blue cheese on the side."

Shay was relieved her mom ordered for her. The last thing she felt like doing was talking, even if it was just to order her food. She realized she hadn't had a freak-out since walking up the bridge on her way from school, but the feelings that came right before it were still there. It was a building sensation that made it hard to breathe and made her want to avoid the thing that was causing it at any cost. It didn't necessarily make sense. She wasn't sure why ordering a salad caused it. She just knew it did.

They passed the menus to the server and she disappeared, leaving them alone. "Mom, where's Alex?"

Her mom looked down and seemed to be searching for the right words. "Well ... he moved out last night."

"What? Are you okay?"

"Yeah. Well ... I don't know. We got in a huge fight."

"You always get in huge fights, though."

"This time was different."

"What happened?" Shay asked, leaning forward on the table.

"I don't really want to get into it with you. Let's just say he made me choose."

"Choose what?"

Mrs. Burke took a drink of the water in front of her. She looked around the table as if trying to find something else to do to avoid the conversation before her. Finally, she answered. "Choose between him and you."

Shay was surprised she'd picked her. She never felt first when it came to Alex. She liked the feeling. "Why would he do that?"

"Because he's an asshole, that's why."

Shay sat back. Finally, her mother saw Alex for what he was. This was the best news she could receive on a day like today. Or really ever.

"So now what?" asked Shay.

"Well, life for you will go on as normal. You'll go to high school after this summer. We'll live in the house. And I'll work at the courthouse. Alex just won't be there telling us everything we're doing wrong and out gallivanting with all the women around town."

Shay's mouth fell open. "I didn't know that part."

"The cheater part, you mean?" Shay's mom had never been so open. "I didn't really want to share that with you. It's embarrassing. I tried to protect you from his issues."

Shay nodded and nibbled on a roll. Bonnie stopped by to top off her iced tea. Shay smiled. "Thank you." Bonnie nodded.

"I can't say I'm disappointed," said Shay. "I just hope you're okay."

"I'm good, honey. This has been a long time coming. But there is one thing you should know."

Shay felt her stomach drop. She didn't want there to be one thing. She wanted to have her fairy tale ending right here where she and her mom lived happily ever after, she aced high school, got into college, and got the hell out of this God-forsaken town.

"What?" she asked, putting her fork down and laying against the back of the booth.

"Alex is going to represent Wayne Garrett. He's the Public Defender and Garrett doesn't have money for counsel." She let her news sink in, then added, "He's threatened to subpoena you to testify."

Shay played with the ends of the cloth napkin on her lap. "That's good, right?" She paused, looking for answers in her mom's worry lines. "I mean, I *can* help put him away for life."

"He'll be up for the death penalty. Alex's job is to prevent that. He'll use you as a character witness for Wayne so he doesn't get the needle."

Shay tilted her head and folded her arms across her chest. "Wait. You mean I would be supporting Wayne Garrett? The same Wayne Garrett that brutally tortured and killed all those women—and almost killed me?"

"Yes."

Shay slammed both hands down on the table, surprising herself and her mom. She wasn't comfortable with the emotion of anger and rarely showed it. Sometimes she felt if she let herself get angry, she would fly into an uncontrollable rage and never be able to stop.

"I won't do it," she said.

"You have to do it if they subpoena you. I know it sucks, but it's not a choice. Alex will try and say that Garrett committed those crimes because he was abused when he was young and he'll want you to confirm that."

Shay looked down and shook her head. Somehow Alex figured out ways to screw her even when he wasn't in the room.

Chapter 15

Litigate
\ 'li-tə-gāt\
verb
to make (something) the subject of a lawsuit: to cause (a case, an
issue, etc.) to be decided and settled in a court of law

The weeks went by with sticky slowness. Shay had imagined a
summer filled with lake trips but going up there wasn't an option. Not
anymore. It had always been a place for fun and adventure, but now it
was just a reminder of those nights with Garrett and the dark side.

She'd thought a lot about it, trying to understand what made Garrett
do the things he'd done, and why he'd treated her one way and Ronda
another. Shay wondered how he'd even found Ryan, but then guessed
he'd probably made it his primary mission. Not to mention the mystery
of how he had seduced Ryan to follow his twisted plans.

Or *had* he seduced Ryan? Maybe Ryan was a willing participant in his
sicko little game. After years of resentment at being abandoned, maybe
Ryan just threw up his emotional hands and snapped.

Shay couldn't shake the inconsistency of how Garrett could be so
chatty and charming as they crossed the lake, then rape and murder a
young girl. But she'd seen what he was capable of with her own eyes.

Ryan. She knew she should be angrier with him than she was. She
wanted to see him, to hear his whole story, to forgive him for what he'd
done. She wasn't sure why. Maybe it was the sheer number of failed
relationships she witnessed around her. Everywhere she looked in
Jefferson, someone was having an affair with someone else. It wasn't age
specific. It was like adultery had rained down on the town in one of the
winter storms and everybody was hit. Her drive to make Ryan work
despite the obvious drawbacks had to do with just wanting not to quit. If
she could just see Ryan, she'd know her play.

Her mom told her that was out of the question, and, outside of
hitching, she wasn't sure how she'd get there without her mom's help.
She sure wasn't feeling overly adventurous after her stay in the caverns.
She didn't trust herself to make the right choices.

And Ronda. She'd gone completely off the grid. She'd stopped
answering her texts. She'd dropped her Facebook and Instagram
accounts. Shay had called the house a few times, but no answer. She

understood that Ronda needed time, but enough was enough. One night at dinner, on a sweltering July pushing a hundred and fifteen degrees at five p.m., she talked about it with her mom over chicken enchiladas and refried beans.

Mrs. Burke scooped an enchilada onto Shay's plate. "Are you excited for high school, honey?"

Shay looked down at her plate and drew a four-lane road through the middle of her beans with her fork. "Not really." She stared down at her creation, then up at her mom. "I haven't even talked to Ronda all summer."

Mrs. Burke nodded. She served herself then laid the spatula in the pan. She sat quietly for a moment before replying.

"I can understand that," she said softly. "You both went through quite a bit."

Shay nodded. "It's weird. We haven't even talked about it."

Shay's mom looked down at her plate and lifted a small bite of enchilada to her mouth. She chewed slowly as if waiting to see if Shay had more to say. She didn't.

"Have you tried to call her, honey? Maybe she's just having a hard time reaching out."

Shay's eyes filled with tears. "I've called. I've texted. I've sent Snap Chat Stories. It's like she left the planet."

With only Shay and her mom at the table, dinner time was so much more relaxed than it used to be. Shay liked that. She didn't like long stretches of silence, though, especially this one. It made her stomach hurt and she didn't want to eat. Then her mom would say, "Honey, why aren't you eating?" and she didn't really know what to say besides "I'm tired" because that's what everybody said when things got too hard to feel.

Shay changed the subject. "How's it going with Alex?" Her mom hadn't spoken much about that at all.

Her mom took a deep breath. "I've been meaning to talk to you about that."

The tone in her mom's voice made Shay wish she'd never asked. There were so many ways this could go. The worst of those was that her mom would say "Alex and I have decided to get back together." She prayed that wasn't it. Even if she had been lonely and missing Ronda all summer, the house had been so peaceful. The yelling and late-night visits had stopped. The thick fogged tension that filled the house had cleared. Shay had found a Yoga show on TV and had learned how to down dog her angst with Rodney Yee. For the first time in as long as she could remember, she was happy to come home. She really would be quite fine if she never had to see Alex again in this lifetime.

"It's about the case."

"What case? Garrett's case?"

Mrs. Burke set down her fork and wiped her mouth with her white napkin, leaving a big red smudge on it from the sauce. She looked down at her lap as she lay her napkin back down, careful to fold the saucy part away from her legs, before looking up, her blue eyes connected with Shay's. Shay saw sadness there. She knew her mom wasn't happy without Alex. She didn't understand why. He'd been mean—a cheater, a drunk, and a child molester—who hadn't treated either of them well at all. Shay's mom at least had a choice in the matter, but for many years, Shay had to numb out just to survive. Levi had been part of that numbing process, Shay realized in that moment. She had used Levi to avoid Alex. She felt the sting of guilt. Scout would never do that when she got to middle school. She'd be stronger than that. Shay decided she would never have a relationship again where she was in it to avoid a more dismal reality. *She* would be stronger than that.

Sitting across from her mom, she held her breath waiting for the next words. She knew her mom needed a man to feel happy, too. It seemed like she believed that a bad relationship was better than no relationship. Shay understood. She'd felt that. But she wished she could be enough for her mom.

God, please don't say he's coming back.

"Yes, well, Garrett's and ours both," she said.

Shay stared at her mom, confused. She wasn't tracking the conversation. She could tell more was coming by the way her mom sucked her teeth as if trying to get a piece of celery out from between them. It was a habit that told she was nervous or getting frustrated. Shay knew she was having a hard time opening up.

She connected. "Your case?" asked Shay. "You have a case?"

Her mom nodded. "Alex and I have decided to file for divorce."

Mentally, Shay threw her arms up in the air, yelled "Yahoo!" She did a little dance in the middle of the table, right smack dab in the middle of the enchilada tray. In reality, she had to tone down her enthusiasm in a display of compassion. It would hurt her mom's feelings to know how much Shay hated Alex, and the last thing she wanted to do was hurt her mom's feelings.

"Oh. Wow," was all she could get out, followed by a polite, "How are you doing with it?"

"It's been tough." Her mom's voice cracked. "At least I won't have to change my name again."

"I always meant to ask why you didn't change it in the first place."

Shay's mom nodded. "I thought a lot about it, but I just didn't want my name different than your name. I didn't want you to feel left out of the family."

That made Shay smile. "Thanks, Mom. And bonus: now you don't have to change all your credit cards."

Shay's mom tried to smile but seemed tired. "That is good news."

The part of Shay that wanted to call in a Mariachi band and piñata to celebrate felt a little dampened by her mom's sullen tone. "What was the other case?"

"Oh, yeah. Well, the two are connected. The other is Garrett."

Garrett had been all over local media. The uproar in Jefferson was so severe they'd talked about moving it to Yolo County, but that hadn't happened yet. Shay had followed the story obsessively, but then had to cut it off all together because it was giving her nightmares.

"What's going on there?" asked Shay.

"You know how I explained Alex is the public defender, right?"

"Yeah."

"And you know he's defending Garrett against the death penalty?"

Shay did know, but she found the whole thing infuriating. Here she was, Garrett's intended art piece, and Alex was going to defend him. Class act. Not that she expected much more from Alex.

"I heard," said Shay, dishing a scoop of enchilada into her mouth. "Probably why Ronda won't talk to me."

"Oh, honey, it's his job," said her mom. "Not to defend Alex, but he doesn't have a choice."

"You *are* defending him—yet again," Shay said sharply, then toned it down. "You guys always tell me that everybody has a choice about everything."

"Yes, but, you know the whole thing about everybody has the right to a defense."

Shay rolled her eyes. "Yes, Mom. I've heard it over and over again while Alex defended rapists and child molesters from the bottom of the well. And now he's going to defend the guy who nearly killed me? I never even want to hear his name again."

Mrs. Burke stayed calm as Shay fumed. "Well, see that's the thing, honey. He's filed a subpoena with the court for you to testify."

"I told you no. I'm not going to testify. He raped Ronda and he would have killed us all if we hadn't gotten away. Then there are all the others he tortured and killed." Shay stared at her mom. "How can you ask me to do that?" She could feel her eyes watering. "I won't do it."

"I understand you're upset, Shay. I do. And I'm not asking you to do this. But we are heading into a nasty divorce and I don't think he's going to do any favors for me. He's not happy about me leaving. I think he may try to use doing this to you to hurt me."

Shay felt her chest heat up. She hated Alex so much. "He can do what he wants. I'm not cooperating." Shay paused. "What does he want me to say, anyway?"

"That's the thing. As I told you before, my guess is he wants you as a character witness.

"A character witness?" Shay thought back to Atticus and the courtroom scene. "You mean to sit up in the stand and talk about his character?"

"Well, Alex knows that you've seen Wayne and his father go at it in front of the blacksmith shop. I'm thinking he'll want to show Wayne is the way he is because he was abused."

"Oh, for God's sake. He usually deserved it because he killed a cat or something."

"Nobody deserves to be abused, Shay." Her mom grimaced. "He killed a cat?"

"Well, kitten. Who kills kittens?"

"Did you see it?"

"No. He told me. He bashed its head with a rock because it was crying, and he didn't like crying. He said it was a sign of weakness and that the weak deserved to die. It was horrifying."

Shay's mom grabbed the top bridge of her nose with her hand and closed her eyes as if to keep herself from crying. "I'm sorry you had to see that."

Shay felt bad. "I'm just saying I want this to be over. I don't want anything to do with it anymore."

"I don't blame you. But if they serve you, you'll have to go and testify. If you don't, they'll arrest you."

"That's ridiculous," said Shay. "It's like they're punishing me for being his intended victim. And don't they have to find me first?"

"Yes. And we can avoid the door, but it's a small town. They'll figure out where you are."

Shay thought the whole judicial system thing was messed up. It didn't make sense that they could force her to testify in his defense. She thought he should get the death penalty, and several times over. He hadn't hesitated to torture and kill other people. They knew he did it, and he had confessed to doing it—her mom said he had—so it shouldn't even be up for debate. Shay's opinion was they wasted way too much time and money in this state trying to decide what to do with this type of criminal.

"Let's play it by ear," said her mom. "Maybe it won't even be an issue."

Chapter 16

sub·poe·na
sə'pēnə/
noun
a writ ordering a person to attend a court.
"a subpoena may be issued to compel their attendance"
verb
summon (someone) with a subpoena.
"the Queen is above the law and cannot be subpoenaed"

When Shay stepped on campus the first day of high school, she was filled with both excitement and terror. She immediately noticed the senior football players across the quad, gathered in a spot near the benches right by the hall that everybody walked down to get to class. They wore their football jerseys and made a lot of noise. They acted like they were completely involved with their funny stories, hitting each other in the biceps and goofing off. Shay was turned off. She felt like they were much more focused on trying to look cool than they were at actually being cool.

She wondered if Ryan knew any of them. She doubted it because they were very different. She was sure she never wanted to date one of them. She wished she knew a way she could avoid passing through the hallway to the main class area so she didn't have to get any closer.

Her eyes scanned the grounds for a familiar face. The groups had formed already on the first day of school: the nerds predictably near the library, non-football jock types near the small gym, cheerleaders in the middle of the quad not too far from the football goons, and the stoners near the parking lot with an invisible circle of smoke surrounding them. Shay spotted Ronda in front of the cafeteria, sitting on the stairs talking to Kailee.

Relieved, she started toward them. It felt like forever since she'd talked to Ronda and she was excited to see her. She felt her stomach tighten. She knew there was a possibility Ronda would just walk away. Seeing Shay might just be too hard after what had happened.

As she got closer, Ronda looked up and saw Shay. She leaned over to Kailee and whispered. Kailee looked at Shay and waved her hands furiously.

"Shay," she yelled. Kailee jumped up, ran over and gave her a big hug.

Relieved to have a familiar connection, Shay hugged her back and asked about her summer. She said it was great: her brother won top bull rider in state and was off to nationals. They'd been all over California with him the whole summer. She ran off saying something about trying to get her locker undone.

There were two legends at Jefferson High School, and time would tell whether they were true or false. One was that freshman boys were thrown into the irrigation canals that squared the campus. The canals were cold and deep. Shay doubted that would happen. The second was if you forget your locker combo, you couldn't get another one and would have to carry all your books around school. It would be painfully obvious you'd forgotten your code and the whole world would laugh at you. Shay was more worried about the second legend than the first, and was reminded that she should try her locker combination before class. Her mom had brought her up to practice and she'd done all right, but she wanted to be sure. 14-24-20. She should practice.

"Aloha, my Ohana," said Ronda, finally standing and giving her a hug. "Where have you been all my life?"

Shay was confused. "Where have *I* been? It's like you fell off the face of the earth."

"I know, I know," said Ronda. "You're right. I went on a bit of a social media vacay for a few minutes. But I'm back now." She seemed good. She seemed better than Shay felt.

"I missed you," said Shay. "I called. You never called back."

Ronda hugged her again. "I'm sorry. My parents sent me to my aunt's house in Bali and I was on strict orders to detoxify. We had to juice and everything," she said. "But I think it worked because I really feel much better. It's either that or the Paxil Mom's got me on." She laughed. "What'd you do?"

"I'm pretty sure it wasn't as good as Bali—or Paxil," Shay said. By comparison, her summer had been a wash and she just wanted to move on without dwelling on it. She hoped to God they'd passed the age where they had to write about their summer vacations. She wanted to leave the topic as quickly as possible. "Hey, walk with me. I want to make sure I can get in my locker."

"Good idea. Me, too." Ronda grabbed Shay's schedule that had her locker and combination on it. "Oh, cool. We've got first period together."

Their lockers were also not too far apart and not too far from first period. They went to Shay's locker first. Shay wanted to ask about Ryan, but she had the sense it would upset Ronda. Maybe if she gave it time, they'd be able to talk about that chapter easier. Ronda linked arms with her and said, "I've got a secret."

"What?" asked Shay, intrigued, and glad to have Ronda back at her side.

"Kyle Foster likes you," she said.

"Who?"

"Kyle Foster. He just moved here from the Bay Area."

"Who moves here from the Bay Area?" She looked at Ronda and furrowed her brow. "I don't even know a Kyle Foster. How could he possibly like me?"

Shay couldn't focus on love right now. She'd had too much of that already. Besides, Ronda had proven herself to be a lousy matchmaker. Her brain couldn't process one more thing. Just remembering her schedule and her locker combination was challenging enough. "Anyway, how do you even know this guy if he just moved here?" said Shay, trying to pretend she didn't see the football players leering at them.

Ronda shot them a smile then turned her attention back to Shay. "Kailee told me. Apparently, he's a rodeo guy. Rides bulls with Josh."

"Oh, fantastic. Just what I need. A bull riding boyfriend. Perfect," said Shay. Sometimes she wondered where Ronda came up with this stuff.

"Wait 'til you see him. You might change your mind."

Shay dialed the code: 14-24-20. It opened. "Cool. Next?" As Shay and Ronda turned to walk to Ronda's locker, they practically knocked over the most beautiful male Shay had ever seen. She looked up at his hazel eyes and thick brown hair swept to one side. He wasn't wearing a cowboy hat, but she could see evidence that the hat had been on at some point during the morning. The usual huge silver buckle combo the local cowboys donned was absent. Instead, Kyle Foster wore a pair of cargo shorts with flip flops and a white T-shirt.

"Hey."

"Hey."

"I'm Kyle. I'm not from around here."

Shay laughed. "No kidding. Never would have guessed that."

"Do you know who I am?"

Ronda piped up. "Of course, we all know who you are. You're the newest Kyle to step on the Jefferson High campus."

"And you are?" Kyle asked.

"I'm Ronda, and this is my best friend, Shay."

Kyle dipped his head at them and said, "Pleased to meet you, Ronda and Shay. I've heard a lot about you from Josh."

Shay didn't know Josh, either. He was a senior this year, so she figured most of his intel must be coming from Kailee. Kailee was not only the school gossip, but she was a Jefferson lifer whose family had been there for generations and was not moving away any time soon—or ever. Shay knew that Kailee would be very comfortable dating her future husband through high school, having babies shortly after, and then counting the days to grandkids. Her life would be full of large Christmas and Thanksgiving feasts trumping all, where the extended relatives would gather at a table for fifty and talk about the town folk. She would start stringing lights for Christmas the day after Thanksgiving and transform her castle into a Winter Wonderland that would end up on the seven top decorated homes list. That was her dream.

"Well, I hope it was good," said Ronda. "You're ahead of us because all we know about you is that you ride bulls with Josh."

"I do," he said. "Maybe you'll come watch me some time." He smiled at Shay and then at Ronda. Shay liked the way he balanced his attention between them. He was polite to both, making both feel equally important.

"That sounds great," said Ronda. "When's your next — what do they call them — gig?"

Kyle laughed. "They just call them rodeos. We moved up here to be closer to the scene. It wasn't as big in the Bay Area as it is in these parts. Y'all love your rodeo up here. The next one is in two weeks in Red Bluff. There's a dance after."

"Cool," said Shay.

"We'll be there," said Ronda.

"Great. I'll snag you some free tickets." He winked. "Got to get to class. I'll see you around. It was nice meeting you, Sha-Ronda." Kyle turned and walked toward his class. Shay was aware that all eyes were on him. Not just the girls were checking out his hot vibe, but the guys were also sizing up their competition. Kyle Foster was definitely the new "it" on campus.

Ronda and Shay headed to Ronda's locker as Ronda giggled, "See? He's so hot. He's totally into you."

"I don't know, Ro. I think he likes you. Rond-yle could totally be a thing."

Ronda stopped and made Shay face her. "Really?"

"I do," said Shay. She decided right at that moment that Kyle belonged to Ronda. Shay needed some time alone to sort out what she was really looking for in a relationship. Take time to sort out her daddy issues. From the time she was small, she had only looked at boys who looked at her first. Somebody would tell her somebody else liked her, then she would decide whether or not she liked them back. She usually did. She could see the good part of most anybody. It seemed easier, and with less potential rejection, than to set her eyes on someone she liked, approach them, and risk that they may not like her back. That was too scary. It all took too much energy. She needed to get whole again — or for the first time. Right now, she just needed to step out of the drama and focus on the steps that would lead her to college.

Jefferson wasn't a college-bound town, but Shay knew she was going. She didn't know how. It wasn't like they had the money. But in eighth grade, the high school counselors came to Jefferson Junior High. Mr. Noroni had A–F, which made him her counselor. He was a tall man, with short dark hair and deeply set dark brown eyes. He asked her what she had planned for after high school. She told him she had no idea, and that was the truth—she absolutely didn't. He told her that she was a very bright girl and that she should take classes to prepare for college. Shay told him they didn't have the money to go. He told her not to worry about that part. "Where there's a will, there's a way," she remembered him saying. Clichéd, yes, but Shay listened. He gave her hope and inspired her to study hard and believe she *could* go to college somewhere other than the local community college, which was where most local people went for a while before quitting.

Something inside her told her they'd figure it out and she'd escape Jefferson. Maybe her mom would move wherever she went, too. Over the summer, she'd thought a lot about what she wanted to do. She knew it would be something that had to do with crime. She could be one of those CSI people, or an investigator who solved crimes like Ronda's dad did. In that way she could turn this whole Garrett thing into something productive. A rainbow in the cloud.

Ronda knocked her out of her daydream. "Cheerleading tryouts are next week. Want to try out?"

"Cheerleading? Really?"

"Why not? You're not doing track, right?"

"I've heard it's hard," said Shay. "And I don't really like running."

"Cheerleading it is. We need something to keep us in shape."

"As if it's a sport," said Shay.

"What are you talking about? It's totally a sport. They work out just as long as any group of athletes. There's strength, coordination, flexibility, and teamwork."

"But do you really want to be known that way?" said Shay.

"We're not going to be *those* cheerleaders," said Ronda. "We'll be the nice kind."

They walked past the football players and into the main hall. "As long as I never have to go out with those Neanderthals," said Shay.

"Oh, come on," said Ronda. "They can't all be bad. Just like not all cheerleaders are bad, right?"

"I guess." Ronda made a good point. She wasn't sure where her judgment of football players came from, but she definitely had one. She needed to work on that. Still, she would be a basketball cheerleader for now.

They walked into AP European History and sat down next to each other. The class buzzed with first day jitters, but Shay didn't see a teacher anywhere. The bell rang and the students quieted and looked around, but her first class of high school was definitely all students. Just as the students were chatting amongst themselves about what was going on, the door opened slowly. In walked a tall man, probably at least six-five, carrying a potbelly he covered up with a lemon chiffon turtleneck sweater. Shay wondered how he stood it in the heat. Over the sweater he wore a brown houndstooth coat with patches on the elbows. His eyebrows were a mixture of black and gray coarse hairs that shot off in all directions and seemed to have a life of their own. He rolled a mint over his tongue repeatedly. His black cowboy boots clicked against the floor as he walked.

"Good morning, ladies and gentlemen. Mr. Max here. Let's start by standing up."

Everybody looked around tentatively, confused by the differences in high school. At middle school, the teachers were always yelling at students to sit down or else. Shay had never had a teacher speak to her so respectfully. In fact, she couldn't remember anybody ever calling her *lady* before.

"We're going to move our desks into a circle so you're all civilized and can see each other. We're all connected in one big circle of life, right? Go."

The students began pushing, pulling, and wrestling their desks into a circle. When the circle was made, they sat.

"The question is," he began. "Is this a desk? Or ... do you just perceive this is a desk and so it is?"

Everybody just stared at him, then quickly looked away just in case he got the idea to call on them and make them answer his unanswerable question. Mr. Max pulled up a chair and joined the circle. He stuck his long legs straight out and laid back against his chair like he'd just finished a long day at the mill. He looked at each student with beady light blue eyes, rolling his mint over and over his tongue, not saying a word. He just sized each student up with a penetrating stare that was just short of creepy. His pant legs hiked up enough to show the stitching on the sides of his black Tony Lamas under the dark gray polyester slacks he wore cinched by a belt under his potbelly.

Awkward silence filled the room as the students sat in the circle looking at him and at each other while he stared back. Finally, he spoke.

"Good morning. You already know who I am and you probably realize that this class is going to be different than any class you've ever taken. We're not going to tell history from the side of the winners exactly. We're going to explore it on a deeper level."

Shay was intrigued. She sat up straight in her seat, finally feeling respected as a learner and a person. That was new for her. Most of her teachers acted like they barely had enough energy to get through the day and were just going through the motions until retirement. Not Mr. Max. He'd clearly given this some thought. He'd made it different from the moment he walked into the classroom. There was something about the way he engaged himself and trusted them as thinkers that excited her.

After another silence, he spoke again. "We're going to go around the circle. You are going to tell your cohort here about your epistemological beliefs. We want to hear your metaphysical explanation as to why you're here. Really, what's more important?"

The students searched for the answer to what the hell he was talking about in each other's eyes. Shay liked his style, but only one class into high school, and she was already entirely confused. She might be in over her head.

"Let's start with you," said Mr. Max looking right at Shay.

Crap. She had no idea what he was even talking about. "Could you define episte- ... episte-?" she asked.

"Perfect response," he said. "It's the ego's trap to think you know everything at fourteen, or even at ninety-five for that matter. We are all learning. If you don't understand something, you ask, just like Ms.?"

"Burke. Shay Burke."

"Okay, Shay Burke. Nice start. So what *epistemology* means is simple. It's the gathering of knowledge. *Metaphysical* is taking a look of what lies beyond the physical. In essence, why are we here and how do we go about finding that out?"

Shay felt her heart slamming against her ribcage. She flashed to her time in the cave with Ronda, wondering if she was going to live or die down deep in the earth without technology to help her, down in those depths where she really had to dig into her internal guidance system. She rolled over various ideas in her mind. She'd never really thought about it. What would Scout say to his question? Scout always had an answer to everything. She thought about Scout talking it over with Atticus in front of the evening fire. She took a stab.

"Well ... I guess we're here to have our own unique experiences and learn from them ... and then we can help other people by sharing what we've learned." She looked at Ronda. Ronda looked down.

"Yes. That's a great start, Shay. But where do we go to gather information to prove this theory or are we just to intuit this to be true? Someone else speak up."

Shay was relieved about the someone else part. A sophomore boy Shay recognized from Jefferson two years ago spoke. "We study history. We look at the great thinkers and writers and people from different

112

times."

"That's right. Experience is key. Observing our own. Observing that of great thinkers. But we also must consider the writer of any particular account. Whose voice gets to be heard and whose are drowned out? Two siblings explaining a missing cupcake to their mother is a perfect example. There are always different perspectives."

The conversation went on as they discussed the metaphysics of existence. Shay was fascinated. She felt for the first time somebody had asked her a meaningful question that she was interested in thinking about. She wondered if it was just a trick and tomorrow they'd be handed a huge list of vocabulary words and dates to memorize on flash cards.

"Why are we sitting in a circle?" asked Mr. Max.

"So we can sing Kum ba ya?" said Tom Costa, a freshman Shay had heard was a smartass.

Some students giggled, but Mr. Max just looked at him until he cast his eyes away. Mr. Max knew who he was. "No, Mr. Costa. There are several reasons. One, it shows the connection—a circle, like the world. Another is that great thinkers have gathered in circles since the dawn of time. Have you ever heard of the Knights of the Round Table? They did not sit in rows and stare up at a board. They gathered together to serve the greater good. So, we study history and why we're here so that we can be better citizens of the world."

Somebody hummed "The Circle of Life" from *The Lion King* and a few students snickered.

Citizen of the world. Shay liked that. She felt like it gave her life meaning, like it gave meaning to the hard things she'd been through— with Alex, with Garrett, with Levi and Ryan. When the bell rang, Shay was disappointed. She wanted that class to go on all day and she couldn't wait to get back tomorrow.

She waited for Ronda to gather her books and walk out with her.

"That class is going to be totally hard," Ronda said. "I might try and drop it."

"Don't drop it. It's going to be great. You don't want to miss something great just because it might be hard."

"I have no idea what he said in there," said Ronda. "What's next period?"

"I have Spanish 1. You?"

"English 2."

They walked down the hall past walls of lockers. Shay spotted Levi walking toward them. He smiled and gave her a nod. She tried to look away but was too slow. He and his goofy grin were bee-lining straight for them. Ronda leaned over, "Don't look now—"

"Yeah, I see him," whispered Shay.

As he came closer, Shay wondered what she'd seen in him.

"Hey, Shay. How's it going?"

Ronda immediately sent him the get-lost arm cross and shifted her weight to one foot. Levi ignored her and raised his hand to touch Shay's arm.

Shay would have preferred to avoid the whole awkward exchange. She didn't want to talk to Levi and she was pretty sure he didn't want to talk to her. She wondered if it would be like this for the next four years where they'd have to make awkward small talk between classes and pretend like they liked each other. She was still angry at Levi for lying to her and making her feel like she was the paranoid one when what she was feeling was right on point. It wasn't even the cheating that was the worst part. It was the cheating and then insisting he hadn't that had fueled her self-doubt.

Now he stood awkwardly in front of her, waiting for a response she wasn't sure she had for him. Finally, she mustered up a "Good. You?"

He took that as an invitation to announce how he'd made the freshman football team and really thought he was the obvious candidate for the quarterback position. That was because he was faster than Mason Davis who hadn't even run track in eighth grade so clearly was not up to speed with what the team needed blah, blah, blah.

Shay wanted to throw up. "Nice. Well, gotta go or I'm going to be late for Spanish." She turned and walked with Ronda right into a tall man trying to pull off a dressy cowboy look. He was dressed all in black and wearing a black felt cowboy hat.

"Shay Burke?" he asked in a deep voice.

"Umm. Who are you?" she asked.

"I'm a friend of your mom's," he said. "Shay?"

"Oh, my God. Is she okay?" she asked.

"Yes. And I need to give you these papers," he said, handing her an envelope.

Ronda looked frazzled. "Shay, I've got to go. I'm going to be late."

Shay nodded. "See you at lunch." She could tell Ronda didn't want to leave but was getting worked up.

"What are the papers for?" she asked.

"Just read them," he said and turned away.

Shay stood still for a minute, watching the man in black walk down the hallway, then stuffed the envelope into her book bag. The bell rang. She ran down the hall to Spanish and went in. The entire class turned to watch her walk through the door. She was suddenly very aware of her first day outfit: miniskirt, T-shirt, and flats. She hoped she looked okay.

"¿Como te llamas, Señorita?" said the teacher. "Me llamo Señora Chrysler."

It's not like she could have walked in late to math or English or any other class where people speak English. No. She had to walk into freaking español and be hit with Spanish before she knew it. And what kind of name was Chrysler for a Spanish teacher anyway? Like the car? At least, she thought that's what she said. She tried to remember her early childhood viewings of *Dora the Explorer.* That could be helpful right now.

"Um. *Me llamo Shay?*"

"*Bien. Ahhh, Señorita Burke. Por favor unete a nosotros.*"

Shay was at a loss, but since Señora Chrysler pointed in the direction of the open seat, Shay followed the visual clues to her chair navigating the snickers of other students. Señora Chrysler went on to announce that all future late students would be invited to dialogue with her in Spanish in front of *la clase.* She talked about how they would allow English until spring break and then it would be an only Spanish-speaking classroom. Only by actually speaking the language would they move on and really learn.

Shay didn't dare open the papers in class, but she was dying to know what they said. Right now, she just wished she could say *adios* this class, and go figure out what the weird man in black had given her.

Chapter 17

yo·ga
ˈyōgə/
noun
a Hindu spiritual and ascetic discipline, a part of which, including
breath control, simple meditation, and the adoption of specific bodily
postures, is widely practiced for health and relaxation.

At the end of Day One, Shay found herself in front of the television
in a down dog position with Rodney Yee, breathing deeply through her
nose and filling up her abdomen. The stress of the day had been
magnified by a thousand thanks to the man in black and her reunification
with Ronda. She was left in an empty house to deal with her stress alone,
and she just needed somebody else there. That's when she found Rodney.

She was happy about seeing Ronda, but the emotions of it were
draining. It was weird that they hadn't even discussed the Garrett thing.
Ronda was sent away breakdown status and then just dismissed it as a
summer vacation. Meanwhile, Shay stayed at home in the land of high
temps and hot tempers as her mom and Alex boxed it out for the house.
Shay had no idea who would win. All she knew was it was just another
mercury notch on the stress thermometer. And although she was pretty
sure Ronda had heard about it, she never even asked.

Then there was the man in black. Shay had opened up the papers and
read the subpoena. It told her she needed to be in court to testify or she
would be held in contempt. She needed to talk to her mom about that
when she came home and figure out what could be done. When her mom
was still not home by six, she and Rodney were on their own.

Following their workout together, Rodney encouraged her to rest for
a few moments in the corpse position. He called it *Savasana* which Shay
thought sounded much better than corpse. He said to clear the mind just
breathe in and out, in and out. When thoughts come, dismiss them. Shay
tried, but her mind jumped around to fifty different scenes. First, she saw
Garrett crossing the lake at night with Ryan bound up on the boat deck.
Then she saw Ronda vomiting into her overflowing bucket. She saw
Garrett leaning over his victim at Dead Man's Rope, blood splatter on his
face. She saw Levi looking at his phone, smiling and turning it over in his
room while saying it was a wrong number. She saw the man in black turn
and walk away.

One scene rolled into the next. Shay wondered how — or if — it would ever end.

Shay heard the garage door. *Savasana* called her to stay. She heard the kitchen door open. Rodney told her to gently open her eyes. She stared at the ceiling, waiting for her mom's voice.

"Well, what do we have here?" said Alex.

Shay jumped up, her heart racing. "What the fuck are you doing here?"

"Now that's no way to greet your daddy, is it Shay Bear?"

"You are *not* my daddy, you creeper," said Shay. "You never were."

"Aw, Shay Shay, come on." Alex walked toward Shay as if he was going to hug her. "We had some good times, didn't we?"

Shay felt like she was going to vomit. "You disgust me."

The kitchen door opened, and Mrs. Burke yelled, "Get the hell out of here, Alex. What the hell? Do I need to get a restraining order now?"

Alex yelled back, "It was my house, too. And I still have stuff I need."

"Like what, Alex? What is it that you need?"

"Not that I need to justify it to you, but I have some papers in the back room —"

"Just get them and get out," Shay's mom yelled.

Alex stomped down the hall, hitting the side of the wall with his fist. "Bitches," he yelled. "Like mother, like daughter."

Mrs. Burke yelled, "Fuck you" at the top of her lungs, then sat down next to Shay.

"I'm so sorry you had to see that," she said in a much softer voice. "I don't know how I ever married that guy."

"Me neither," said Shay.

Mrs. Burke cocked her head to one side and looked at Shay, "You never really liked Alex, did you?"

Shay wasn't sure when Alex was going to pop back out of the hallway. She wondered what was taking him so long. She whispered just in case. "Didn't like him? I *hated* him."

"Hate is such a strong word, Shay. Do I need to tell you about the toothpaste again?"

Shay sighed. "I know, I know. Easy to squeeze out into a big mess, but nearly impossible to get them back in once it's out."

Shay's mom smiled. "Good to know you were listening. Let me go see what the hell he's doing." She stood up and headed toward the hall, just as Alex was walking out.

"Got what I need," he said, and waved a file in the air.

"Good. Now get the hell out and don't come back."

They watched him walk through the kitchen and reach for the door, then pause and turn. "So Shay — see you in court." He quickly left, leaving Shay and her mom in an open-mouthed staring contest.

"What's he talking about?"

"I've been waiting to tell you. Some big guy dressed in black and a cowboy hat brought me this envelope today after first period. He said he was a friend of yours."

"Pete Shafter. Bastard."

"I didn't know what it was and he made me late for Spanish so I couldn't open it. It was awful. I had to talk in Spanish in front of the whole class."

"I'm so sorry, honey. Where are the papers?"

Shay's backpack was nearby with her assignment from Mr. Max to write an essay on how she viewed the world. She pulled the envelope out and handed it to her mom, who pulled the papers out and scanned them, shaking her head.

"That bastard," she said, and folded them back up.

"Does it mean I have to?"

"I'm afraid so."

Shay grabbed the papers back and opened them. "It's soon."

"And during school, which really sucks. I'll have use a vacation day to take off work, which is about the last way I'd like to spend a vacation day."

"Not like I want to take a day, either," said Shay.

"I know, honey. I'm sorry."

Shay lay back on the floor, took a deep breath through her nose, filled her abdomen, and held it. She counted to ten in her head. Then she let it out slowly through her mouth counting backwards from ten. Smell the cupcake, cool the cupcake. Smell the cupcake, cool the cupcake.

When she was done, she sat up and looked straight at her mom.

"I can do this," she said.

***

Shay woke up the next morning to the unforgiving blare of her alarm going off over and over again. She'd heard it in her dream, but in her dream, she thought it was an alarm warning of danger up ahead. In the dream, she'd found herself rushing down a muddy river swirling in circles on an inner tube. She loved tubing down the Jefferson Creek when she was younger, pressing flat against the tubes so the overstretching irrigation pipes didn't take her out. She and her friends would spend the entire day floating in the sun, butts sunk down in the cold creek water, waiting for the next rapids.

But the dream rapids were different—more violent. They swirled in circles around protruding boulders and the river was wider, faster, and more frightening than the gentle current of the creek. Two tubers were with her, but they were spread out. She couldn't tell who they were, but she knew they were friends. In the dream, she moved from the observer's position on the shore to a rider's position on the tube. From the observer's position, she could see that the creek was on a down slope, moving toward a waterfall drop. An alarm sounded as if the tubers had passed some invisible barrier and triggered the blare. Shay had never been so relieved to have the sound be her alarm clock and not a warning sign she was about to die.

She thought about the dream during first period when Mr. Max brought up the idea of perspective. He said a story is told differently depending on the storyteller's view point. In her dream, she'd seen the river from both perspectives. On the shore, the river was beautiful, with lush green foliage falling down into it and blue skies shining down on the white-capped water. The swirls were hypnotizing, and the tubers looked like they were having fun. From inside the tube, though, Shay felt out of control—dizzy with danger. She felt the fear of the unknown for her and her friends.

Life was like the river, swirly at times, muddy and hard to understand. People came in to ride with you and then they jumped out. Sometimes, there were waterfalls that could pull you into them and kill you, and at other times you could just observe the power and beauty of that waterfall from afar. At one point or another, you'd be in both those positions.

The next few weeks were filled with cheer tryouts, Rond-yle love, Shay and Rodney Yee love, and buzz about who is going with who to homecoming. It seemed incredibly insignificant to Shay when she thought about Garrett, a guy not that much older than she whose life hung in the balance.

He had done horrible things that Shay couldn't believe or understand. He had bad things done to him as well, but nothing seemed proportionate—at least that she knew about—to the crimes he had done. And yet he'd spared Shay. She wondered if that was just luck, or if it was because her work here was not done. She didn't know the answer. The personal connection confused her even further.

She did know one thing for sure. She was dreading getting up on the stand and testifying in front of Garrett and Alex and a whole bunch of strangers inside a courtroom.

She also didn't know how she felt about outcomes. A huge part of her believed he deserved to die. He'd brutally murdered all those women and savagely attacked many more. An eye for an eye. But she wasn't sure it was right to decide who lived and who died. That seemed to her to be the same thing that Garrett had done. Maybe it would be better if they just kept him locked away forever, but somehow that didn't seem harsh enough. Not to mention that everybody else would have to foot the bill for his lifetime stay. As much as she hated Alex, and althouth she'd never admit it, Shay was starting to understand different perspectives and why it was important for a person to be represented. Even if he was a scumbag.

Chapter 18

tes·ti·mo·ny
ˈtestəˌmōnē/
noun
a formal written or spoken statement,
especially one given in a court of law.

Shay's mom parked the car on a hill north of the courthouse building. The building seemed too fancy for the area. Grecian white columns and deep steps led up to the white front. The vast lawn in front of the courthouse was green and lined with beautiful trees in reds, oranges and yellows. The leaves had started to change early. It reminded Shay of the colors that lined the road to Crystal Creek when she used to travel there with Mama Mae to visit Garrett at his first detention camp. A man in a gray suit sat on the bench, smoking a cigarette and talking angrily on his cell.

They entered through tall double doors and stood behind lawyers taking their shoes off. They emptied pockets, taking everything out. Shay's mom motioned her to follow suit. Shay put her bag in the holder and pulled her cell from her pocket. The lawyer in front of them mumbled with the guard about not understanding why she needed to do this every day since he full well knew who she was. They had known each other since Kindergarten. The guard nodded in sympathy.

"I know, Marcia. Hands are tied. You know the rules," he said.

"Stupidity," she grumbled as she slid her pumps back on. "I'll send you the bill for my nylons that keep getting holes from your rules."

He laughed. "You do that, Marcia. You do that. Not my rules."

"Next." The security guard looked Shay up and down. "No school?"

"Well … yes," said Shay.

"That's where she'd rather be, believe it or not," Mrs. Burke said in an effort to get the ball rolling. Rupert had a reputation for taking his time and she knew it.

"Well, hello, Felicia. This your daughter?"

She nodded. "This is Shay. Shay, Rupert."

He gave Shay a big smile. "Nice to meet you, Shay. Looks like you got the whole family up here today, huh?"

Felicia's puzzled face prompted Rupert to follow up. "Alex came through early this morning. I'd barely signed in."

Felicia Burke cringed. "Alex and I are in the middle of a divorce, Rupert."

He shook his head. "Sorry to hear that." He made a sad face at Shay. "The kids always lose."

"Not this time," said Shay, slipping her shoes back on her feet. "Really." She smiled and walked toward the elevator with her mom.

"When we get to the courtroom, I'll go in and check you in. You won't be allowed to sit in while other witnesses testify," Shay's mom said.

"Who else will be speaking?"Mrs. Burke hit the button to the second floor. Shay noticed her hand was shaking. "Expert witnesses. Maybe Ryan."

Shay looked at her. "Ryan?"

"I'm just guessing. I mean, he was a huge part of it, right?"

Shay looked at the floor, all of her mixed feelings swirling around in the small space. "I don't know. I mean—I guess."

The elevator door opened, and Shay and her mom walked into a wide, open hallway with shiny gray linoleum floors. The sound of Shay's heels clicked against the floor. She hated wearing heels, but her mom said she needed to wear a crisp white shirt, black skirt, and black pumps for court. Shay felt like she should be taking an order at a table in a steak house or something. The clicking echoed through the oversized hall which gave it an eerie feel. They walked in silence down the hall to a bench outside Room 222, Honorable Judge Alice Small presiding.

"Wait here. I'll check us in with Judge Small's constable." She opened the heavy wooden door and left Shay in the hall alone.

Shay hadn't been too nervous until her mom stepped behind the large door. She bounced her legs, trying to keep her knees together. She wished she had some of Ronda's meds. The current that flowed through her felt electrical. It made her feel like she was going to have one of her freak-outs. She hadn't thought about those since the day she'd escaped from Garrett. Through the whole cavern escapade, she hadn't had one, and now she felt it could happen at any minute. What would really suck was if it happened while she was sitting in the witness stand in front of Alex, Garrett, and whoever the hell else was going to be in there.

No. She would not allow that to happen. This was where she turned into SWA: Shay with Attitude. This is where she channeled that precocious little Scout and pretended Alex was Atticus. She was no victim here. She would do her part and that was that. She stopped her legs from bouncing and placed her feet flat on the floor like Rodney told her to do in Mountain Pose. "Feel the roots shooting down into the earth," he said. She felt it. She definitely felt it.

Her mom peeked out of the courtroom door. "They're ready for you, honey."

Shay stood up and put her shoulders back. She took a deep belly breath and walked in. She surveyed the room. In front, stepping down from the place she recognized as the witness stand from all her *Law and Order* marathon sessions, stood Ryan.

He froze mid-step and stared straight at her. His hair had grown longer and hung in his face. He smiled warmly at Shay and mouthed, "I'm sorry."

Shay nodded and smiled, mostly with her eyes. Their lives could have turned out so differently. Ryan could have been getting ready to come up with a clever way to invite her to the prom. They could have gone to the mall together to pick out matching tie and dress color combos. She knew Ryan liked her and she felt he truly was sorry. She would never be able to trust him again, but she forgave him. She didn't regret the kiss in the caverns, either.

He stepped down and followed the man in front of him who seemed impatient and irritated by his glance in Shay's direction. Judge Small sat back in her chair closely observing the interchanges between all the players. She looked at Shay's mom and nodded a "hello," along with a raised eyebrow which indicated, one, she knew Felicia Burke and, two, she wanted to know why Felicia's daughter was making googly eyes at a co-defendant. Shay couldn't wait to get the hell out of this small town.

They sat down on a bench as Ryan was escorted out of the court room through a side door. Judge Small looked through some papers then up at Alex.

"Defense, call your next witness."

Alex stood up. "Yes, thank you, your Honor. We call Shay Burke to the witness stand. We'll have her sit before we bring in the defendant."

Shay shot a glance at her mom and whispered, "He's coming?"

Shay's mom shrugged and patted her leg. "You've got this. Just tell the truth."

Shay stood, taking a big breath while she walked through the swinging wood door, in between the defense and the prosecution tables, and up to the witness box. She stepped up.

"Wait right there Ms. Burke," said the Judge.

The bailiff walked up with a Bible and stood in front of Shay. "Place your right hand right here, Miss."

Shay did as she was told. Her hand was shaking.

"Do you swear to tell the truth, the whole truth, and nothing but the truth so help you God?"

Shay knew to say "I do," and she tried, but the words got stuck. She cleared her voice and made another attempt. "I … I do."

"You may be seated."

Shay sat in the witness stand and looked out at each table of lawyers, then back at her mom. The court room looked scary from here, but Shay was determined to remain strong.

"You may bring in the defendant," said Judge Small.

The doors in the back swung open wide and Wayne Garrett lumbered in. Shay felt the air in the room shift. Her shoulders tightened. Her stomach felt nauseous. She wondered if her legs would go numb. She wanted to turn her eyes away and not stare, but she was transfixed by this person they were calling Garrett.

He was not the same Wayne Garrett Shay had known. His eyes were glazed over, like the real ones had been plucked out and glass ones popped in their place. He cast them down at the floor about twenty feet in front of him, apparently looking at nothing in particular. An orange jumpsuit covered his limbs and torso from top to bottom. His ankles were bound by thick chains that clanged as he shuffled his feet. His wrists were crossed over in front and connected with shiny silver handcuffs. His brown curly hair parted in the middle and dropped down past his shoulders. It was greasy and thin, making his acne-covered face look pale and drawn.

The detail that most hit Shay was the swastika that had been carved on his forehead. It was a deep, ruddy red and looked like it had to have been done by somebody other than Garret himself because of the angle. Shay wondered if he'd given the designer permission or if they'd just taken it in an Aryan moment.

The bailiff navigated the swinging gate so that Garrett could walk through and get to the table where Alex sat thumbing through a thick file. Shay'd been briefed about what was going to happen, but they'd left out the part about Garrett walking in looking like Charles Manson jacked up on downers. Shay felt her knees bounce in rapid time and was thankful they were hidden from Alex. She refused to show him any weakness. Instead, she would plow through this testimony, confident and honest, and in the end, justice would prevail.

She surveyed the court room. Judge Small sat on her right. She wore a long black robe that blended with her black shoulder length hair. She had a calming aura, which Shay needed. Down in front sat two tables, the one on the right with the district attorney whom she recognized from cocktail parties her parents had hosted. She'd hated those cocktail parties. Everybody would show up all polite and nice, but by the end of the night, they'd be sloshed and telling gross jokes loud enough for the neighbors to hear. Alex made her his trophy kid. Her job was to pass snacks around and recite poetry.

The party host himself sat at the table on the left. Next to Alex, a junior attorney, fresh out of law school. She looked slender in her black suit and high heels with the obligatory crisp white shirt poking out underneath the jacket. Blonde hair, short and choppy with a little too much product for Shay's taste, completed the look. Shay was pretty positive Alex was sleeping with her by the way he leaned into her, laughing and whispering.

Straight in front sat the court reporter. This woman would take down every word she said, words that would forever live in Garrett's file until the end of time. No pressure.

Judge Small made some comments that Shay couldn't process. Then, "You may begin," with a nod in Alex's direction.

"Thank you, Your Honor," said Alex with a goofy grin Shay guessed was supposed to be charming.

"Now, Shay. There's nothing to be nervous about."

Shay wanted to smack him. Her anxiety morphed into anger. His condescending tone and need to act like Father of the Year made her want to vomit right there all over the floor. She stared at him.

"Do you understand, Shay?"

The judge gave her a look that nudged her to respond. Shay leaned forward to talk in the microphone. "I understand." She hoped it didn't sound like she was clenching her teeth as she said it.

"Atta girl," Alex said. "Now, I would just like you to describe your time at Mr. and Mrs. Garrett's house when you and Wayne Garrett first got acquainted."

Shay flashed back to the fields and the blue tarps. She flashed to laughing and playing in the irrigation fields like sledders in the snow, but with the warm sun dancing off the wet grass. She remembered the good times, the early adventures with The Daycare Kids when nobody cared what time it was. She missed that freedom. She wasn't sure what Alex wanted. She only knew she didn't want to give it to him.

"It's okay, Shay. Don't be afraid, honey." Alex smiled his politician grin, giving the court reporter a wink. "Let me rephrase."

Shay nodded and leaned forward to the microphone as if she was trying really hard to come up with a response. Garrett continued to stare down at the floor in front of him, his lips parted just enough to make him look like he was completely drugged out. The difference in his appearance made Shay unable to look away entirely, but she didn't want to stare, either. Even after all he did, she felt overwhelmingly sad for him. What a waste of a life.

Alex moved closer to Shay. "Tell the court about the first time you witnessed Garrett Senior beating up little Wayne." Alex stared at Shay with eyes that said *and make it good*. "Just tell us what age you were."

Shay cleared her throat. She was confused about how to answer. Wayne's dad wasn't the one beating Wayne up as much as they were fighting each other. In fact, Wayne often threw the first punch. The way Alex worded his sentence was deceptive. She needed to set the record straight.

"They were *both* fighting," said Shay.

Garrett looked up for the first time and glared at her, but in an unfocused way

"Yes, we've established that," said Alex. "But my question was—and if you could just answer the question, that'd be perfect—how old were you the first time you saw them fighting."

Shay's jaw tightened, and her stomach hurt. "Four ... maybe three."

"Good," said Alex. "So basically ten years ago?"

"Basically."

"Great. Can you describe who was with you when you saw the fighting?" .

"The Daycare Kids. There were three or four of us there," said Shay.

"And is it true that The Daycare Kids used to make bets on who would win the fights?"

Shay hesitated before answering. "Yes."

"Did you make bets on who would win?"

"I thought it was mean, so no," said Shay.

"And while my client's dad was beating him up, what else were The Daycare Kids doing?"

Shay didn't understand why The Daycare Kids were on trial. "They were cheering on whoever they bet on. His dad was a lot bigger, so most people bet on him."

"So basically, a bunch of kids were standing nearby, cheering on Mr. Garrett to beat little Wayne up?"

"Well, not—"

"Yes or no, Shay."

"Yes."

"And did you ever witness any other violence against my client? For example, did you ever see Mr. Garrett whip my client with a belt?"

Shay hated the way Alex spun the story to make Garrett seem like the victim. Everybody had dysfunctional family issues, and many people are abused, but they didn't all then go out and rape and murder five women and attack others.

"I never saw that," said Shay.

"But you knew it happened?" asked Alex.

"Yes."

"How did you know it happened?"

"I saw him take off his belt and then I heard Wayne screaming from the other room."

Alex paused for effect. "Did you ever see the marks on his body?"

"Yes."

"Where were they?"

"All over his back."

Alex paused and walked back to his table. He flipped open his folder and looked inside. Shay knew he was not going to even cover the part about how Garrett had tried to pick her up. That would be completely counterproductive to what he was doing here. Or worse—irrelevant. Her almost-murder, in Alex's eyes, was irrelevant.

The jury listened to tales of how Garrett was abused in most violent ways, how Mama Mae had spent all her time with The Daycare Kids and neglected Garrett, how he felt unwanted by the original adoption and never got over it. The circle of life and the cycle of violence. It was inevitable.

The thing was, Garrett had an older sister—also adopted—and nothing of the sort had happened to her. Shay never knew her, but she'd heard Mama Mae talk proudly about how she'd gone off to college and become a nurse.

Alex approached Shay again. "I'd like to thank you for your time, Shay. You did great." He reached out his hand to help Shay out of the box, a gesture to show the jury what a gentleman he was, no doubt. Shay ignored him. She stepped down. She passed between the tables two feet from Garrett, who'd returned his gaze to the floor. She hurried down the aisle between the benches and through the large wooden door into the open hallway, her mom following behind. She fell on a bench with her hands on her face and sobbed.

Even though Shay'd only been on the stand for a short time, she felt like it had been a lifetime. The prosecutor hadn't had too many questions for her, and she was grateful for that. She hoped she'd never have to come back to this courtroom again.

Her mom sat down next to her rubbing her back. "You did great, honey."

Shay couldn't speak. So many emotions swirled around her throat wouldn't even work. She wondered what would happen to Garrett. She hurt so deeply for the families who'd lost their loved ones that way. She hurt for Mama Mae, who'd adopted this son whom she loved as much as any parent loves a child. She was proud of herself that she'd survived testifying without having a freak-out on the stand. Alex had manipulated her words, but she'd stood strong and didn't buckle. Alex might not be Atticus, but in that moment, she felt Scout's strength. She promised herself she'd never let that go.

Chapter 19

Intoxication
Noun
in-ˌtäk-sə-ˈkā-shən
an abnormal state that is essentially a poisoning

When Shay got to school, Ronda wanted to know everything. She knew Shay was going to testify and she wanted to make sure Shay helped to "get that bastard the needle." Ronda had testified the day before, and the grueling experience had shaken her to her core. On cross examination, Alex had been, as Ronda described it, "a complete dick."

Shay didn't have the courage to set her straight and explain that if anything, her testimony was meant to prevent that. She also couldn't tell her that she'd talked with her mom about timing and knew that it would probably be at least a decade before the execution—if the verdict was for the death penalty.

As they sat on the benches in the quad at noon, drinking grape juice and eating chocolate chip cookies, Ronda needled her for information.

"Was it totally creepy?"

"Yes." Shay didn't even know where to begin to unravel the levels of creepiness.

"Did Garrett like lunge at you or anything? Fucking bastard."

"No lunging. He looked like he was completely drugged up. He looked different."

"Different how?" As Ronda spoke about Garrett, her dark passenger came pushing its way to the driver seat of the conversation. Shay understood. Garrett had totally violated her.

"Just really sad. And out of it." The image was burned on the back of Shay's eyelids, and she wanted nothing more than to replace it with butterflies and puppies. Something. Anything but Garrett. "There was this swastika thing carved in his forehead."

"What?" Ronda asked. "Like the nazi thing?"

"Yeah. I don't know. It's not like I discussed it with him or anybody else. His hair is also really long. He looked a lot like that Charles Manson guy from when our grandparents were young. Have you ever seen that dude?"

"Nope."

"Well, Google him. That's what he looked like." Shay never wanted to talk about it again. Ever. "So, what's going on with the dude? You going for it?"

Ronda smiled. "We're going to homecoming."

"No way. How did he ask you?"

Ronda giggled. "He made me a sign that said 'If you go with me to homecoming, it'll be the ride of your life.'"

"Ew."

"No, not like that! He drew a bull and a cowboy holding on to the reins."

"Oh, okay. Better. Cute."

"And then when I said *yes*, he turned it around and it said 'Hold on Tight!'"

Each year, proposals to homecoming had reached a new level in the creativity department. Each ask tried to outdo the next. Shay was pretty sure nobody had tried the bull riding metaphor.

"We'll give him an A for originality," said Shay, just happy to be talking about something other than Garrett.

"You should come—to Homecoming, I mean," said Ronda.

"I don't have a date, and, frankly, I don't want one," said Shay. At this point, she just needed to take a week-long nap.

"Come with us. We're going to a great party after at Zak's house."

With all the heaviness of the divorce, the trial, high school, and Ryan, a party sounded like a good diversion. She'd never been to one.

"Don't you think I'd be a total third wheel," asked Shay. "How would Kyle feel about the whole thing?"

"Here he comes. Let's ask him," Ronda said, smiling at Kyle moving toward them from across the quad.

He walked up, grabbed Ronda's grape juice, took a sip, and said, "Hey, ladies. How's it going?"

"Great, but we have a question," said Ronda sheepishly. That was funny because all Shay ever saw was a loud, aggressive Ronda around guys. The way she was acting was completely new.

"Shoot," said Kyle.

"How do you feel about Shay going with us to the dance—and to Zak's first?"

Kyle smiled. "Me, with the two best looking ladies in school? Hells yeah." He linked arms with Shay on one side, Ronda on the other, and said. "Can I walk my ladies to class?"

Shay wondered what she'd gotten herself into.

***

The afternoon of Homecoming, Ronda and Shay decided they would spend the night at Shay's house. With Alex gone and Ronda still having trouble sleeping in her room, it seemed like the best choice. Shay's mom was out a lot, and they might even have the house to themselves.

They spent the afternoon primping. They sat out in the sun, painted their nails, and put on mud masks. They put mayonnaise in their hair because Ronda had read in *Teen* magazine that it was a great deep conditioner. Ronda had brought over Margarita Mix and tequila from the cabinet, which was easier and easier to pull off since Ryan was gone. Her parents fought all the time when they were home together, and her mom had started leaving tequila bottles hidden around the house.

They followed the directions on the blender, mixed the Margaritas, and drank them all afternoon. Shay had never felt as giggly as she did that day with Ronda. It was such a contrast to the experience they'd had in the caverns. In fact, the cavern felt like a dream, and the more Margaritas Shay drank, the less she remembered the caverns.

Twenty minutes before pick up, Shay and Ronda threw on their prom dresses and shoes. Kyle pulled into Shay's driveway, right on time, and they watched him walk up to the door. He looked handsome in his black button up shirt against black pants. Not everybody could rock the look, but Kyle pulled it off. He had two bouquets of white roses in his hands. Shay and Ronda giggled and went to greet him at the door.

"Ladies," he said. "For you." He added, "You both look amazing."

"So do you," said Ronda .

Shay added, "So handsome."

Kyle escorted his dates to SUV, putting Ronda in the front and Shay in the back. "I took my dad's car so one of you wouldn't have to ride in the back of my truck," he laughed.

"Thoughtful," quipped Shay.

They headed to Zak's house down I-5. "You guys excited?"

"Of course," said Ronda, slurring her words a bit.

"Have you guys been drinking?"

"Just a few margaritas," said Shay, which threw both her and Ronda into non-stop laughter for a reason she couldn't quite figure out.

"Guess that makes me designated driver," said Kyle. "That's my job tonight."

"You're a good guy," said Ronda, reaching over to grab his leg. "We're so lucky."

When they pulled into Zak's, cars were lined up and down the road. Shay couldn't believe how many were there. Kyle pulled into a spot behind a beat-up blue Chrysler and parked.

"Allow me," he said, getting out then walking over to open the doors for Shay and Ronda.

"Thank you, kind sir," said Shay, stepping out onto the dusty gravel in her high heels. Already wobbly, the heels were like stilts. Ronda was having the same problem.

Kyle had a girl on each arm and walked up the walkway. The door to Zak's house was cracked open and they could hear music piping out.

"Hey, look who's here." Zak stepped out and gave Shay a big hug. She had recently met him in Spanish. They loved to pretend they could speak Spanish, but really all they could ever remember was "¡Usted es muy feo y gordo!" They thought that was hysterical and it had become their daily greeting.

"¡Usted es – muy Hermosa!" Zak said to Shay, changing it up.

"¡Y usted es muy guapo!" said Shay. "You know Ronda and Kyle, right?"

"Of course! I know everybody. Come on in. Keg in the back. Bong in the living room."

When they walked in, Shay could barely see through the smoke. The room was full of people she'd seen on campus but didn't really know too well yet. It didn't matter, though. She felt like they were all there on even playing ground to forget about the stresses of their lives. It didn't matter here what your grades were or who you knew; it was just about chilling out and having fun.

Kyle saw a friend from English and started talking to him. Ronda stood next to him. Shay followed Zak into the backyard to see the pool. With everybody all fancied up, she was pretty sure nobody was going in, but it did make for a fancy backdrop.

"You want a shot?" asked Zak. "We've got a shot table back here."

Shay wanted whatever would clear her mind of Garrett. "Sure," she said.

They walked to the table and Zak took a big bottle and poured it into two tiny shot glasses. He handed one to Shay.

Shay took the glass. Zak clinked his to hers then downed it. Shay copied him. She thought her throat was on fire.

"Shit," she said. "That burns really bad."

"Only the first few," said Zak. "The first one is always the worse."

He poured two more. "¡Otra vez, senorita!"

Shay drank another, and another. She started to notice it was getting harder to talk. "What is this stuff?"

"Sloe gin."

"Why slow?"

"Because it hits you slow and hard."

And it did. Suddenly the giddy feeling Shay had felt turned into a feeling she didn't like at all. It felt almost identical to a freak-out with the added bonus that she felt super nauseous. She put her arms out to steady herself.

"You okay?" said Zak, taking another shot.

"I don't feel so—" Before she could say *good,* Shay puked all over the pool deck. Vomit ran down the front of her dress.

"Dude!" said Zak and a collective "Ew" sounded from around the pool. Shay felt it coming on again so strong she couldn't stop it. The force of the vomit made her pee at the same time.

"Shay," she heard Ronda call her. Ronda came over and helped her into the bathroom. Coming back out, she said to Zak, "I've got to help her get cleaned up—can we borrow some sweats and a bedroom?"

Shay spent the rest of the night passed out in Zak's spare room while everyone else went to Homecoming. In the morning, Zak made coffee and apologized for the sloe gin thing. He didn't realize it would hit her that hard. Shay's pounding headache and dizzy head convinced her that sloe gin was not the fast ticket to forgetting about Garrett. She'd need to find another way.

Chapter 20

Execution
Noun
ek-si-ˈkyü-shən
the act of killing someone especially as punishment for a crime

Ten years later.

Shay walked to the third story window and opened it wide, letting in the salty beach air. She loved the smell of ocean filling up the condo. She loved how the sea sparkled in the sunlight. A swim in those waves was next on her list after she finished the last chapter that never seemed to end. It would be good to celebrate the completion of that. The cool Pacific waters would be her reward. She sat down at her desk, her eyes searching the horizon for the words she needed. Just when she found some, the phone rang.

Shay looked down at caller ID and hoped everything was okay. Her mom usually called on a predictable schedule and this wasn't it. "Hey, Mom."

"Hey, honey, you busy?" Her mom's voice sounded weird.

"Just staring at a blank page." She pushed herself back from the screen and put her feet up on the desk. "Everything okay?"

"Yes. Is now a good time?"

"Yeah, Mom. What's up?"

"Honey, I don't know if you've been following the news on Garrett. Have you?"

That name. Shay hadn't thought about that name since forever. She'd shoved it down into the darkest corners and slammed the door. It was much easier to pretend the whole thing never happened than to invite any of it to her new life.

"Not so much, Mom. It's not on the news down here." Shay breathed deeply. Spring in Southern California brought the jasmine bloom and every so often she'd catch that scent. It calmed her. "It's hard for me."

"I understand. Well, I wanted you to know they've decided his fate. He's going to be executed."

Shay placed her feet square on the floor and held her breath. She should feel relieved. Part of her did. Another part felt sad. Still another, elated. All the same feelings she'd had from the beginning. "When?"

"Soon. The death penalty in California is very wishy-washy. One minute it's legal and the next it's not. A bill was just passed making it legal, and, because of the circumstances, they want to move quickly."

"It's a lot to process." Shay stared out the window and spotted dolphins playing in the distance. She wanted to join them and forget about everything else. She loved her new life here in Redondo Beach nestled in Southern California's South Bay. She didn't want to let this old part seep in.

"I know it's a lot, honey," said her mom. "I know this is quite a struggle for you emotionally. It might be healing to go." She hesitated. "Do you *want* to go?"

That sounded horrible. Why would anybody *want* to go? Shay couldn't even imagine wanting that. But something inside her overruled all those thoughts and answered for her.

"Yes."

"Okay, great. I think it'll offer closure. You want to fly into Sac and we'll drive out?"

"Sure, Mom. Sounds good."

"Let's talk later."

Shay hung up the phone and plopped herself on the couch, her focus on her mom's last words: *I think it'll bring closure.* She stared at the ceiling, wondering if her mom was right. So much had happened since that time back in Jefferson when Garrett had terrorized her small town. It seemed like lifetimes ago. When she thought back to her fourteen-year-old self, Shay did not like what she saw. That Shay was weak, always aspiring to be like Scout, but so far away from what she perceived Scout to be. Her obsession with the fictional character felt strange now, but she suspected it had perhaps flowed over from full up-to-the-brim daddy issues she'd had. Those issues lead to choices she saw now as lame. It was hard to forgive herself for being so needy.

She felt different now at twenty-four. Stronger. She'd found her voice in words on the page, through endless journaling and story writing. She understood now that Scout was a character created by a writer, perhaps out of Harper Lee's own aspired-to values. In real life, people were often far more complex than even the best-written characters. Each comes with some form of pathology, sometimes obvious and sometimes hidden, and each is thrown into an environment that at times they can't control. That environment matters, but so does how one responds to it.

Shay thought a lot about nature versus nurture and which carried more power. She'd long contemplated whether Garrett was born bad, what some called pure evil, or was molded by a set of traumatizing circumstances that made him traumatize others. Part of her didn't care.

She hated him for what he'd done. Part of her wondered if somebody could have done something along the way to prevent that all from happening. Her mom was right. This might be the thing to give her closure.

***

A week later Shay's mom picked her up at Sacramento Airport and they drove south to San Quentin's Death Row where Garrett would be executed. The excitement Shay felt seeing her mom was wiped out with a recurring wave of hate and anger when she thought of Garrett. The effect he'd left on the town. The pain he'd caused Mama Mae, who'd been such a kind caretaker to him and to Shay. The brutal attacks on those women who he'd tortured and savagely killed. The ones he left to live with and try to move past what he'd done.

She couldn't hold it in. "What he did to those women—to everybody," said Shay. "It's unforgivable."

Felicia Burke looked at her daughter as they passed by rows of oleanders along Interstate 5. She seemed ready for this conversation. She nodded. "He had to be in a great deal of pain to cause so much in others."

"He deserves to die," said Shay. "Only it's not as cruel of a death as he gave all those women. That doesn't seem fair."

"I know what you mean," said Felicia. "But many times, holding onto anger just ends up drawing out its power over you." She paused, groping for the right words. "It's complicated."

"And yet it's pretty simple, really. I'm glad it's finally going to be over."

Shay's mom passed the car in front of her. "See that's the thing, though. Is it? Is it really over?"

Shay stared out the window at the rows of almond trees that passed by as they drove south down Interstate 5. The blooms formed rows of fluffy pale pink in the spring. "No. I don't think it will ever really be over. It's one of those things that stick in your mind forever."

"Yes." Shay's mom drove in silence for a few minutes. "I'm not sure what to share or not share with what's been happening at the prison."

Going to this event was supposed to help with closure, her mom had said. It was a term she'd gleaned from her new therapist. Shay wanted to try.

"Let's get it all out in the open. And then let's see if we can close the book."

Her mom reached over and touched her arm. "Good, honey. For one thing, reports say Wayne has reclaimed his original heritage. He says he's a quarter Cherokee. He calls himself Young Elk. He's been trying to get

Alex to get him permission to go to the sweat lodge before the execution for spiritual atonement."

"Seriously?" Shay wondered about all the other women and their rights to atonement.

"Yes, but I don't think it'll be allowed. There are rocks and shovels in there. It's too dangerous considering his violent background and penchant for rocks."

Shay turned to her mom. "Do you think a person can atone when they've done something like this?"

"It's such a hard question. There are two different viewpoints and you'll see both represented today."

"I think it's obvious," said Shay.

"I used to think so. But one group of people say that executing someone—taking their life—is doing the same thing to them they did to someone else."

"Well, that's ridiculous," said Shay. "Nobody's raping him and throwing him off a bridge."

"No, that's true. In fact, he gets a last meal of his choosing and a new outfit for his execution. I'm just glad we're not paying for him for twenty-two years then killing him. That's how it used to be in the past."

The drive was a little over two hours from the airport. Shay and her mom talked about old memories at Mama Mae's, both good and bad. They talked about the pain of all the different people that Garrett's story had touched. They talked about what happens when someone dies. Shay's mom had read somewhere that one of Veronica's relatives said that "Garrett better hope there's not an afterlife, and if there is, he'd better hide." Shay totally understood.

What they didn't talk about was Ryan, although he was certainly on Shay's mind. Ryan had turned State's witness and testified against his brother early on in the trial. His cooperation resulted in a plea bargain with minimal time and a lifetime of community service, and most likely a shorter trial than would have resulted otherwise. Ryan had testified *in camera*—in a closed courtroom—due to his status as a minor defendant, but rumors flew wide in the small town. According to one, Ryan had claimed to have been forced by Garrett to do what he was told under the threat that more people would be killed if he didn't. But the truth that wasn't grist for the rumor mill was that the manipulation had started one night soon after Julia's murder when Ryan was drowning his sorrows out at a lake party. Garrett approached and befriended him. In Ryan's emotionally distraught state, it was easy. He told Ryan they were brothers and he'd wanted to meet him for most of his life. Ryan's raw pain welcomed the new balm, and, in Garrett, he felt he had made a new friend to fill the hole losing Julia left.

Over the next few days, Garrett continued to exploit Ryan's vulnerability. Garrett told him he needed his help. He confided that he was working on a project that had involved Julia. When Ryan realized that Garrett had killed Julia, he tried to figure out a way to break free, but Garrett threatened to kill his family. And after Shay ended up in Ryan's shed, and he began falling for her, Ryan knew he would have to stay involved to protect both Shay and his family. Ryan was ultimately moved to Folsom to serve out his sentence.

Shay tried her best to push him from her mind.

When they pulled into San Quentin, the guard notified them the whole prison was on lockdown for the execution. Protestors out front carried signs. Family members walked toward the chamber. Shay and her mom parked and followed. Native American drummers filled the air with rhythmic beats. Shay's heart pounded her ribcage.

They filed into an apple-green viewing chamber where they waited. Some people cried. Some sat silent. A man in skull and crossbones T-shirt sat expressionless. After some time, Garrett walked in. He wore a blue shirt and blue jeans. His hair had been shaved and the swastika no longer looked as pronounced.

A man strapped him to a gurney. As he lay with his arms and legs secured, with a fourteen-inch ritual white feather with black edges draped on his chest, a solution of sodium pentothal was pumped into his veins to render him unconscious. The man who injected the first shot then administered a second. Shay's mom explained this was to paralyze his diaphragm and stop his breathing. The final shot would paralyze his heart.

Throughout the execution, Garrett lay very still with his eyes closed. Once he swallowed and his cheeks seemed to bulge. In the final moments, his face turned slightly purple.

But the thing that stuck with Shay the most from that day, the thing she would never forget, was his last word. As he lay strapped to the gurney, the white feather on his chest, Wayne Garrett spoke his final word: "Peace."

Author's Note

Time is a distorted lens. Sometimes we think we remember what happened. Other times, we can't remember anything at all. Then there are those times we remember in a crystal-clear way that will never blur even when we wish it would.

All are valid. The beauty of the novel format is that it allows these true events to inspire story without demanding that distorted lens be adjusted in a certain way that is often impossible to do. Do consider this while reading this novel.

The true events that inspired this story remain in the forefront of my mind today. I think it's because they hold synchronicity at such a level that's always perplexed me. When I was six, I started going to a babysitter named Momma Lil. She was married to Daddy Dean and they had two adopted children, Sharon and Darrell. I never met Sharon because she had moved before I started going to the house for babysitting. Darrell was a different story. I spent quite a bit of time at the Rich home growing up. There, I developed a love for Worldwide Wrestling and the *National Enquirer* magazine which Momma Lil read to me like bedtime stories. I'm happy to say I've given both those up.

I formed a bond with Darrell. He played with me in the irrigation fields and haystacks on the long hot summer days. Five years my elder, I looked up to him, even crushed on him at some points. He protected me in a way I can't explain, but deeply felt. As we aged, I sensed a shift in him that pushed him out of reach. He grew distant and angry. I watched him and Daddy Dean in fist fights, and it hurt me deeply to see people harm each other so intentionally in that way, especially someone I cared about. I was aware Darrell had started to get in trouble because my stepdad was a criminal attorney and defended him, though from what I wasn't sure. It got worse as he aged until, finally, he was placed in a camp for young juvenile delinquent boys. I always wondered what went wrong.

Momma Lil would go visit him on Sundays and take me with her when I was staying at her home. The depth of a mother's devotion always struck me. I remember the drive up the canyon vividly. Towering leaves dressed in deep reds, oranges, and yellows, made shiny by the rain, hugged the upward climb to Crystal Creek. The vivid beauty etched itself in my young brain and I have sought it out on Autumn country roads ever since. I felt sad Darrell was at this camp beyond the colors, but I hoped when he got out, he'd be better. I hoped they would help him.

Instead, he got worse. When I was fourteen, he tried to pick me up on my walk home from school. I felt him before he was there. When my eyes met his, I knew something was very wrong, and that this was not the same person I once knew. Later that night, he picked up his last victim, cornering her in my small hometown's post office. He violently sodomized and bit her young body, took her to the dam, and threw her over while she was still alive. When I found out, the whole situation hit me so deeply I pushed it down and didn't speak about it again to anyone. I think that was true for most of my town.

How do I reconcile the Darrell I once knew with this brutal version? The murders and attacks he made on these women and children were—I can't even find words that connote the level of depravity. The trajectory of witnessing him over the years still confuses—and sickens—me to this day. For each of his victims and their loved ones, I feel such compassion and empathy.

When Darrell Rich was caught and brought to trial, my stepdad and my mom were going through a caustic divorce. My stepdad was one of the defense attorneys for Rich, which I did not understand at all. He subpoenaed me as a witness to the beatings Darrell endured from Daddy Dean, but said not one word about the fact he had tried to pick me up or what he'd done to young, sweet Annette. At the time, the move felt like it was done to spite my mom, and I was a pawn in the game. I was warned to only answer what was asked. It was terrifying and I went to a place of numb to get through it all. When I stepped off the stand, I vowed to put the whole thing behind me, which I did for about thirty years. I did not speak about it to anyone, not even during the execution.

However, synchronicity is a dance partner with surprising moves. She leads a turn when least expected. It was 2008 and my family had newly relocated to my hometown. I was re-writing my novel *First Break* for the umpteenth time in a local coffee shop. A man kept showing up at the same time I was there, and we began to talk. One thing led to another and eventually we started talking about my next book, *Intuition*. It was this story that had haunted me since I was young, before I moved away, and when I returned, so did it. On the way home, I would pass by Darrell's house each day, the home I'd slept in and where police eventually found his killing kit in the closet. It turned out my coffee shop friend was the lead detective on the trial and, as we talked, many other details I'd suppressed rushed back.

The threads of our lives, Darrell's and mine, crossed in very strange ways. He was executed at San Quentin three days after my 36th birthday on March 15, 2000. I found out that he had been born in the same small beach city hospital in Torrance, California, albeit years before, where both my babies were born and from where we'd lived a mile away in the South Bay of Los Angeles for fifteen years. He'd been both my protector and my near predator, which taught me that life is not always black and white, and often complex.

He'd also crashed his motorcycle in his teens and sustained what I know now to be traumatic brain injury. Today, we understand that TBS manifests in many ways we are only currently beginning to understand. From what I know now, I suspect he was also experiencing a psychotic break. We depend on our internal GPS, our intuition, to sort these things out. But what happens when our intuition becomes damaged? For me, my intuition saved me that day in June. For Darrell, he was running some different operating system I simply didn't understand. To this day, people share pieces of this storyline I never knew, and the stories continue to teach me the complex nature of humanity.

Additionally, we know now that early childhood adversity experiences (ACES) left unaddressed are a public health crisis. The ACES scores in Shasta County where I grew up continue to be the amongst the highest in California. Whether high ACES, mental illness, some other pathology or a combination was behind Darrell's unraveling in such a chaotically brutal way, we'll never know. All we know is many lives were tragically affected, people were harmed in unspeakable ways, and decades later many are still affected by this dark period in small town history.

That brings us to current day. I see all the technology we use each day and how it often distracts from our intuitive navigational systems. I wondered what it would be like to have experienced that summer of '78 in current day, where everything is immediate and moves so much faster. That's where my intuition led me, and I have learned to trust that above all else. That is why the story is contemporary, to reimagine the influence of technology.

In prison, Darrell discovered his Native American heritage and embraced it. Because he killed many of his victims with a rock to the head, a final sweat lodge request was denied.

Indeed, his last word during his execution at San Quentin was "Peace."

About the Author

 Jamie Weil lives in Cottonwood, California. She writes everywhere and in a variety of mediums. Jamie has identified as a writer since third grade when her teacher sent her poem "Red" to the *Record Searchlight* and they published it. She has written books for children and teens, as well as the adult non-fiction market. She has also worked as a journalist, law firm marketing director, second grade teacher, and professional mom. She owns a production company called Balsamic Moon Productions, LLC and is currently writing and co-producing/directing a docuseries called "A Crazy Thought," a six-part series focusing on youth and reframing mental/brain illness (www.acrazythought.com). Her first novel, *First Break*, is a companion piece to that docuseries and tells the first-person story of coming of age during a first psychotic break. You can find out more about what Jamie's up to here: www.jamieweil.net

ALL THINGS THAT MATTER PRESS

FOR MORE INFORMATION ON TITLES AVAILABLE FROM
ALL THINGS THAT MATTER PRESS, GO TO
http://allthingsthatmatterpress.com
or contact us at
allthingsthatmatterpress@gmail.com